The Gr

How the Trouble Started

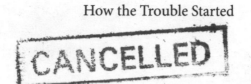

by the same author

Luke and Jon

How the Trouble Started

ROBERT WILLIAMS

faber and faber

First published in this edition in 2012
by Faber and Faber Limited
Bloomsbury House,
74–77 Great Russell Street,
London WC1B 3DA

Typeset by Faber and Faber Ltd

Printed in the UK by CPI Group (UK) Ltd, Croydon CRO 4YY

Extract from 'Think of a world without any flowers' by Doreen
Newport (1927–2004) © 1974 Stainer and Bell Ltd, 23 Gruneisen
Road, London, N3 1DZ, England, www.stainer.co.uk. Reproduced
by permission

A CIP record for this book
is available from the British Library

ISBN 978–0–571–28854–0

2 4 6 8 10 9 7 5 3 1

Once again, for Kate

1

The police were involved over the trouble. They had to be. But I didn't think of them as the police at first. As an eight-year-old boy I expected uniforms, flashing lights and handcuffs. Speeding cars and the glimpse of a gun. Instead there was a tired-looking woman in a business suit who drove a grey car slowly and always smelt of coffee. She told me to call her Tracy, but I'd never called a grown-up by their first name before and couldn't bring myself to do it. I tried, but it felt as impossible as saying 'fuck' in front of my mum, or jumping off a wall that was too high. I teetered on the edge a few times but my brain wouldn't make my mouth form the correct shape and I ended up calling her 'Miss' instead. 'Tracy,' she said, the first few times, but after a while she shook her head and gave up.

There wasn't a knock at the door until the evening of the day it happened. I'd been expecting repercussions, I should be clear about that, but I didn't expect those repercussions to be an interview at the police station. They asked a lot of questions but I didn't say too much. It wasn't that I was scared, they were nice enough, they didn't shout or anything, but I didn't want to get into more trouble and the more I spoke the more trouble I might get myself in, so I went quiet. 'I was just playing,' I told them, but that wasn't enough. They kept going back to the beginning and tried to work out every second of everything that had happened that morning. I started to get dizzy with it. I don't think I lied to them and whilst they didn't quite lie to me, they didn't tell me the whole truth for a while either. I suppose they were trying to work out if I was hiding anything, testing how much I knew, but even at eight years old I knew not to say too much, I knew words could get you into trouble, words could trip you up. But I wasn't up to being devious at eight, I didn't have it in me then. Mum thinks I've grown into deviousness since, and maybe she has a point, but back then I wasn't devious, I was just careful.

When it became clear that I was missing something important, that things weren't quite as I understood them to be, I had one question to ask. But when I asked it everyone in the room ignored me so completely that I wondered if I'd spoken the words out loud. I waited until there was another chance and asked again. It drew the same non-reaction from everyone. It was either later that night or the next day when they did their big reveal. I can't remember all of the details from those early days, but I do remember what I was wearing when they told me. It was summer and I had blue shorts on and my school shoes. I felt daft in shorts and shoes, but they'd taken my trainers away with all the other clothes I'd been wearing when it happened. I was taken to a bare room with green plastic chairs and a grey table in the middle. They sat me down and told me the answer to the question I'd asked twice previously. Tracy spoke slowly and clearly and everyone in the room was watching me closely like I was a magician about to do a trick. I listened to what she had to say and tried to understand it fully. It was a hot day and when she lifted her hands from the table she left a flurry of damp patches in front of her. I watched them disappear, Tracy finished talking, and they all looked at me, waiting for me to say something, so I said the only words I could think of to say – I asked when I would get my trainers back. It was like I'd dropped my pants and waved myself about. Everyone looked away and Mum started to cry and somebody said, 'Bloody hell, he's a cold fish isn't he?'

Mum sat me down that night and told me I wasn't making a good impression of myself. 'You need to show some compassion Donald.' I promised I would try harder. The next day I was back in the room with the green chairs. We all settled down and Tracy asked more questions. She wanted to know what I understood by 'intent'. I listened carefully whilst she explained. 'It's important for us to know what you *meant* to do Donald, what you were thinking in the seconds before it happened and why you did what you did afterwards.' She used the word 'intent' a couple more times but in my eight-year-old head I was only reminded of the night me and Matthew Thornton camped in his garden, his mum and dad taking turns to check on us from their bedroom window. I think they knew we wouldn't last the night, and they were right, and we abandoned the tent an hour after it went dark and slept in bunk beds in his bedroom, happy to be safe indoors. That was all 'intent' meant to me back then. I tried to explain that I didn't *mean* to do anything at all – that I was just playing outside and it went wrong. But Tracy wasn't sure. She seemed to think there was something I wasn't telling her, that I was keeping from her information she needed to know. As I've grown older I've come to understand that there is something about me people don't trust, and even as an eight-year-old I wasn't convincing. Eventually they decided there were no more questions and we didn't have to go back to the police station again. The next day I was back at school.

That was that, except I was taken out of class once a week and driven across town to a place called *The Happy to Be Here Centre*, where I went into a room with a woman called Karen and played for an hour. At the time I didn't think it was strange, I didn't think about it much at all; I was just happy to get out of lessons and play. There were some rules – you went in empty-handed and left empty-handed. If you wrote or painted anything, that had to stay in the room in a box with your name on it. And your mum wasn't allowed in, so it was just me and Karen. It drove Mum mad that she had to wait outside. She didn't trust me and she didn't trust them. 'What do you do in there?' she asked.

'Just play,' I told her.

'Well, play carefully,' she said. And I tried to play carefully, but I'm still not sure to this day how you're supposed to do that.

There were puppets, toy animals, toy cars, a doll's house, model soldiers, teddy bears, and paints and paper. Sometimes I played with the toys, sometimes

I painted. Karen would join in and do a picture too. She would tell me what she was planning to paint and then ask what I was painting. When I was playing with the toys she left me to it and watched. She sometimes asked what was going on in the game I was acting out and I would happily tell her.

'The tiger has eaten the soldier's friend so the soldier is hunting him through the doll's house to kill him for revenge. He will wear a tiger's tooth around his neck in honour of his friend.'

Probably something daft like that. I had no idea at the time that they were observing me. Seeing how I ticked. Seeing if I strangled the dolls and stabbed the teddy bears. It was understandable I suppose, but it seems a bit sneaky, spying on an eight-year-old when he thinks he's just playing.

*

The kids at school didn't say anything on the morning of my return, but they must have been told not to, because there was a buzz of not saying anything everywhere. I'd only been off for a few days but the place was crackling with excitement. Mrs Walsh made everyone say, 'Welcome back Donald,' and I was aware of my fellow pupils' eyes on me, checking

6

to see if I looked different somehow. Their eagerness to question me was straining their jaws, I could tell, but it was hard for them to get a chance. Even in the yard it wasn't going to happen – there were twice as many teachers on duty as usual, and whilst they normally stayed close to the doors with their hands wrapped around coffee cups, on my first day back they circulated and crisscrossed the yard like Scalextric cars around a track. It wasn't until lunch break that anyone got close. The Hudson triplets must have clocked me on my way to the toilet because two seconds after the door swung closed, it banged open and before I even got my hands to my zip they were in front of me, a mini-army, jostling, asking, 'What happened? Did you go to jail? What did your mum say? Was there loads of blood?' I didn't get chance to say a word before Mr Barker burst through the door and chucked us out and made us walk off in different directions, ignoring my plea that I really did need the toilet. The school's vigilance persisted, and looking back I think it was a shame how they went about it. Of course the kids were interested, but we were all made very aware that it wasn't something that should be discussed before, during, or after school. The school was trying to look after me I think, at least partly they were, but it didn't really help. Everyone knew what had happened and everyone was wary of me. And then, when I did finally get back to being friendly with Matthew, my only real friend before all the trouble, he was pulled aside and they checked that he wasn't asking anything he wasn't supposed to. Pretty soon I became the boy you got into trouble for talking to.

*

For a while I wasn't sure that anything too terrible had even happened that day. I had the suspicion that I was being tricked. As far as I was concerned when I jumped on my bike and raced home I wasn't leaving the scene of anything momentous or dreadful. I knew something bad had happened, I knew someone was hurt and I might get into trouble, but I had no idea that the police would be involved. And when Tracy told me what the outcome had been, that seemed impossible and didn't sit with my understanding of any of it. I didn't believe them and I was at that shadowy age where I'd realised not everything grown-ups say is true. I'd had years of tales about Father Christmas, Tooth Fairies and carrots helping you see in the dark, and all of it turned out to be nonsense. And what I'd been told in the police station in Clifton seemed as far-fetched as a fat man in a red suit coming down chimneys with presents for all the children everywhere.

*

It was important for me to go back to where it happened. To see if there were any clues confirming what I was being told, or anything there to bolster my belief that I was being misled. Something as terrible as they were claiming couldn't happen without evidence left behind, I was sure of that. But it was going to be tricky; I hadn't been allowed out of the house alone since it happened. I did go out with Mum, but I was steered out of the front gate and turned ninety degrees to the right, walked up the hill, away from where it happened, no matter that we needed to go down the hill to get anywhere we needed to go. We would walk up Hawthorne Road for about a quarter of a mile, cut through an eventual side track, and then walk back down Kemple Street, avoiding the house where the trouble happened. It added a good twenty minutes onto all our trips, but I knew not to risk saying anything. Even when I was tired and we approached the fork in the road where one option would have us home in five minutes and the other would send us on a trek out of our way, I kept shut. Since the day the police had arrived at the door Mum had been prone to crying and anger in equal measures, and I was learning anything I said could provoke her. I was learning it was best to keep quiet. Words can trip you up.

I arrived at a plan. I would wait until Mum got herself to bed and then let myself out of the house an hour or so later. I would run down to where it happened, have a good look around, and see if I could find any evidence to support what they were saying. But on my first attempt I found myself being woken up for school in the morning; I'd slept through the whole night. The same thing happened the next morning, so when Mum was in the bathroom I had a rummage around in the drawers and cupboards in the kitchen and found an old plastic cooking timer, shaped like a chicken. When I heard Mum go to bed that night I set it for an hour and stuffed it under my pillow. Sure enough I fell asleep, but I woke when the muffled ringing vibrated underneath my head. I turned the timer off and crept out to Mum's door. I listened carefully for any noise and when I heard a gentle snore I knew I had my chance. I didn't bother changing; I wouldn't be too long. I snuck out of the house in my pyjamas and school shoes, a torch in my hand.

It would only have been about midnight but it was a dark night, darker than I'd ever seen, and the street where I'd grown up looked as unfamiliar as when it was covered in a thick layer of snow. The stillness of the scene shocked me and brought me up short at the front gate, I wondered if I would be able to disturb it, but within moments of pulling the gate closed behind me I was a dark shadow, quickly working my way down the black and silent road. Five minutes later I was at the bottom of the hill, outside number five. I shone my torch on the pavement. I was looking for blood. I moved the beam left and right, in the road, along the kerb. I tried further up and further down, in case I'd misjudged the spot. But there were no dark patches of dried blood anywhere. I flashed my torch over the gate and shone the beam up the path to the front door. Nothing there either. I couldn't understand it. There must have been blood left behind if what they were saying was true. I turned my attention to eye level, to see if there were any clues there I could find. I did a full, slow turn. Straight ahead was the junction at the bottom of the hill that took you either into Clifton or out of Clifton. Across the road stood a row of tall, grand houses with steep steps to take you up to their wide front doors. Back the way I came was the long climb

11

which led to my house. And then, the final turn, and in front of me, the house where the little boy lived. No clues anywhere that I could see. It didn't appear to me to be the scene of a tragedy of any kind. I started to get excited then, to believe my hunch that the adults were trying to pull the wool over my eyes. I was about to head home and climb into bed and think it over some more when I noticed the cards in the window for the first time. One of the cards had fallen against the window pane and was twisted round. I would be able to read what message had been written. I'd had no intention of going up to the house before, but I knew it was important to see the words in that card. I opened the gate as quietly as I could and snuck up the path to the window without setting off any alarms. I shone my torch at the black glass, leant in and read:

Dear Becky and Ian,
With Deepest Sympathy
There will never be the words.
He sleeps with the angels now.
With all our love,
Emma, Chris and Imogen

It became real in that moment. I still didn't understand how it had happened, but I believed that I'd been told the truth. I turned to head down the path, to walk back the way I'd come. I took one step and a light popped on above me and illuminated the front garden like a stage. If I'd run and kept running I would have been away in seconds, but in my panic I ran to the middle of the garden and stopped. I turned and considered running back to the house to hide against the wall. In that moment of indecision, when I was frozen to the spot, as obvious as a tower on a hill, the curtains pulled back in the upstairs window and the little boy's dad was there. In the middle of his garden, staring back at him, stood the boy who'd killed his two-year-old son two weeks before. He looked astounded. Then I ran.

2

I changed after the trouble. Mum says that I went
into myself. I see it as the opposite – that I escaped
myself. I called it 'vanishing' and quickly became
good at it. The first time I tried it was just a few days
after the police had talked to me for the final time.
I can see now, looking back, that for a first vanishing it was quite ambitious. But back then I had no
real idea what I was up to; I hadn't the understanding
of a vanishing that I have these days. At the time I
just wanted to escape Mum's upset and the darkness
that had descended on us since the day the police
knocked at the door. The idea came from an author's
visit to the school. He talked to our class about his
writing and his books and I didn't like him or his
stories much, but one thing he said stuck with me.
He told us that he spent his days in other worlds. He
said that when he started writing and inventing the
everyday world disappeared, and when it was going
well he ended up somewhere that felt more real to

him than the world he woke up in. I wanted some of that for myself, I wanted that magical escape, and whilst I couldn't get the words down onto the page like he could so easily, I was good at disappearing to other worlds in my head.

The first time I tried it, my bed was a spaceship and I went to Neptune. I was space-crazy in those days – the books I'd been borrowing from the library were all about space, the pictures I'd been drawing in the play room at *The Happy to Be Here Centre* had been planets, stars and spaceships, and any film or programme that was set in space was likely to get me excited for days. I remember there was a school trip booked to a famous telescope, the Pilchard Telescope, where they said you could see other solar systems if the conditions were right. I was counting down the days, but in the end we moved just before the trip and Mum wrote me a note to take in on my last day, asking for the money back. I'd never known disappointment like it, and it seemed to me probably illegal to build a child's hopes up so high before dashing them like they were nothing. I was sure that someone in authority would step in at the last minute and make it right. When they didn't, and I finally realised that I really wasn't going to see the giant telescope and far-off solar systems I let my displeasure show.

'Good God Donald, this better not be about a telescope,' Mum said. 'After everything that's happened you'd better not be mourning a cancelled trip to see a big daft telescope.'

That's exactly what I was mourning though. I couldn't understand how she didn't see the injustice of it – the only boy in the class who was desperate to see space was being dragged away from any chance of ever seeing it, whilst his classmates, who weren't even half as bothered as him, would be getting on the coach in a couple of days. It seemed to me a miscarriage of justice of epic proportions. Now I shudder at how upset I was. I'd killed a little boy a few weeks before and there I was crying about a cancelled trip to a telescope. But it meant more to me than that. The idea of space was a comfort. The thought that these planets existed so far away from daily life, that I could be sat in class at school whilst these huge bodies of rock and gas were up above me, travelling through space, was something that fascinated me. It was so foreign to everything I knew, so alien to everything down here, that it helped make everything seem unimportant. *Nothing that happens down here ever makes any difference to anything up there* is what I was thinking. And thinking like that helped make life more manageable. That was why I was so upset when my place on the trip was cancelled. I couldn't explain it at the time though, and my behaviour was taken as further evidence by everyone that I was nothing but a cold fish.

Neptune was the planet for me. I don't know why. I enjoyed aspects of all the planets, but Neptune was the one that won my heart. Other planets were enjoyed, maybe even courted for a while, but when it came to it, when I had to nail my colours to the mast, it was always Neptune. Maybe because it was blue; blue was my favourite colour, three my favourite number. I'd done my research. I knew about spaceships and I knew the training astronauts went through. I knew the food they ate, how they went to the toilet, where they slept. I was fully prepared. I was so excited about my plan that I went to bed half an hour before I had to. I lay there and couldn't wait for night to kick in and the room to turn from shadows to black so I could count down to lift-off and blast away. The lift-off went without a hitch and soon I was out of orbit and cruising. I waved at the planets as I passed. Jupiter was as impressive as I'd read, the rings of Saturn spectacular. And then, eventually, I saw the blue crescent of Neptune drift into view and my journey was almost complete. For the next few nights I relived the trip and each night I was keen to get to bed. For however long it took me to fall asleep I escaped Clifton, everyone in it, and everything that had happened. I would get into my pyjamas straight after tea and be impatient until bedtime.

'Is everything all right Donald?' Mum asked after a few days. Everything was fine, I told her, I'd just been very tired lately that was all. She looked like she'd remembered something and said, 'They told me that might happen. It's completely normal Donald so don't worry.'

I knew what she was referring to, but I had no idea why the trouble would make me feel tired. I let her think that she'd stumbled into understanding though; I was happy to keep the vanishings to myself.

The vanishings have changed over the years. I'm no longer as interested in space travel for one thing, so they tend to be more grounded these days, more realistic. Lossiemouth will be the next attempt. I found Lossiemouth on page ninety-six of the *Times Atlas of the World*. It's a tiny white dot on the map, nothing else, but all you need is a name and a destination and the rest you invent. I try to get the details right, I look in books at the library, but it doesn't matter too much, nobody will be testing and as long as you have a good idea of who you are and where you're headed, it normally works out. For Lossiemouth I've imagined a small white cottage overlooking the sea. The town is quiet and safe – there are no boy racers throwing their cars down tight, busy streets, nobody rushing anywhere. In the cottage there is a kitchen table, made by my own hands, the plastering and electrics done by me also. There is a pale blue boat rocking in the harbour, a sheepdog waiting behind the front door and a wife: a tall brunette with a wide red mouth and a gentle smile. My name is Jack and I'm not too tall and I don't have daft muscles, but I am strong and handsome. But when the women of Lossiemouth smile and flick their hair, I pretend I haven't noticed – I'm just walking my dog along the beach before tea, that's all, just living my life. I always remember that I have a beautiful wife waiting in the cottage, waiting for my return, and I always return. Since the trouble they've been good to me, my vanishings. They've helped keep my head above water, helped me to breathe more easily, help me escape the little boy.

3

It was the week before the trip to the Pilchard Telescope and a few months after the trouble when we
left. I don't know why Mum chose Raithswaite, we
didn't know anybody there, and I'd never heard her
mention the place until she told me that was where
we would be living. But she probably had leaving in
mind from day one, and the incident in the garden
at midnight didn't help matters. After that night, and
another visit from Tracy, Mum was constantly
checking where I was in the house, making sure I
hadn't snuck out to be somewhere I wasn't supposed
to be. I'd tried to explain what I'd been up to in the
garden, but she didn't understand, and thought I'd
gone insane and couldn't be trusted not to torment
the parents of the little boy I'd killed. When she told
me we were moving I didn't understand why, but
back then I had the black-and-white understanding
of a child: it was an accident, the police had let me go
and I'd promised never to go back to the house again.

Why did we have to move? But Mum said it was impossible to stay. I didn't believe her at the time, but I wasn't old enough to understand, I wasn't even old enough to realise that girls were worth looking at. Now I can see that she was right – we had no option but to leave. The trouble upset her, I could see that, but I've always suspected that leaving Clifton hit her harder. She really did love the place. She used to say it was the town she'd grown up in and the town she would die in. She sorted the plot at Waddington Road Cemetery just before we left. It was her last phone call. 'At least I have that to look forward to,' she said, 'that one day I will go home.' At the time I didn't think it was an unreasonable idea that she would be able to move back when I no longer lived with her, but when I put it to her she told me that it was a ridiculous notion, that she would never be able to return to Clifton alive. 'What if I see them Donald? What if I see the family? Have you considered that?' She shuddered at the thought of it and I understood then that as far as she was concerned, when she went home she would be cold and they would lower her into the ground.

She never put it to me directly that I'd ruined everything but it's an understanding that's clear between us. It's evident when she bangs pans away into the cupboards with as much volume as she can muster; it's there in her furious mopping of the kitchen floor, which she swears can never be got clean. She hasn't made a single proper friend since we moved to Raithswaite. She hasn't even tried. She rebukes all comers and wallows in her suffering. Everyone and everything in Raithswaite is tainted as far as she is concerned. Everything is dirty. She thinks we ended up in a filthy town. If she could she would take her mop to every street. 'Cramped, dirty and crumbling' is how she described it on the phone the other week to Aunty Sandra. 'This house is just about the cleanest thing in the whole place.' It's not true. When it comes to Raithswaite Mum is like those skinny women who look in the mirror and only see fat. I've tried to reason with her but the truth doesn't suit her thinking so she keeps it buried. She will hide the sun behind a penny coin if it helps her story to do so. And that's a big difference between us. She sees the world as she wants to, I try to see it as it is. I've come to understand that I sometimes misjudge, but I am willing to at least have a proper look, to try and take a balanced view of the world and the people in it.

4

For now the world is Raithswaite and there aren't too many people. There is Mum, of course, and Fiona Jackson from school, I sometimes see her down in the old quarry, but I've fallen between the gaps as far as friends go and there isn't really anyone I hang around with. I'm one of the few sixteen-year-olds who isn't out and about on a Friday and Saturday night. The day this started I'd spent the previous night dreaming about the little boy. I've never forgotten, not for a second, but during the last eight years there have been bad times and better times. There have been days, sometimes weeks, when I've managed to think of it as a tragic accident, that fate had her way and there was nothing to be done. When I'm doing well I'm able to cut my thoughts off like that, before they dive too deep. But on a bad day, in a bad week, I can't forget that I killed someone – I see the stark truth of the matter and it floors me. A single thought can stop me in my tracks, make my blood run cold and steal the breath from my lungs. It wasn't quite as bad for the first couple of years, but as I've got older and begun to understand more, it's been harder. And lately it's been bad day after bad day, no respite, and I can't even remember what happy or glad feels like. I know those feelings do exist, but I can't see that I'll ever find my way back to them. On a stinging cold winter's day, when it's so cold your teeth are hurting, your fingers are numb and you can't feel your own face, you *know* you were uncomfortably hot four months before, but you can't remember what that actually felt like. That's how far away from happy I've been.

I'd slept badly, dreams had cast a shadow, and I'd woken too early for the mood I'd woken into. More sleep was the only way to deal with it, but sleep was hiding anywhere other than behind my eyelids, and there was nothing to do other than get up and face the day. School was closed for an inset day and Mum had forgotten and was annoyed at the thought of me around the place. The irritation buzzed off her and up through the floorboards and I knew that even if I stayed in my room and did nothing I would do it in a way that would provoke her. And after the dreams my chest was tight and panic was hovering in the corners of rooms, waiting to pounce. It was hard to breathe and I needed air. I needed to escape. I left by the back door and wandered towards town. I wanted to put some distance between me and the house and Mum. I really wanted to put some distance between me and myself but that's a tricky thing to do, and the closest I could get to it was walking. I've been doing it for years, walking around Raithswaite, finding out where all the tiny backstreets lead to, walking to the fringes of the town and seeing what's out there, trying not to think about the little boy, trying to disappear somehow.

The sun was bright and kids from school were already out and about, in pairs or groups, planning and nattering, enjoying the free day. The odd shout came my way from across the road, from up on a bridge, but it wasn't having any effect. My brain was caught up in its thinking. I ended up at the cricket ground at the end of Chatburn Road. I wandered around the pitch and noticed that it wasn't even close to being properly flat and I wondered how they ever got a decent game out of it. As I continued on I started thinking about why the latest vanishing hadn't worked. I'd planned Lossiemouth to the last detail. I had the house and the wife and I could see it all clearly and easily, but when I tried to disappear, it didn't work. I've planned less and had more successful vanishings in the past. It was a worry that recently my brain was unwilling to be tricked.

The day was warming up and heat was easing over my body and working its way through to my bones and I was thinking that at least something felt good. I was coming up to the scrubland at the bottom of the cricket pitch, just beginning to relax a little, when a man flew past me on a bike so close his jacket toggle nearly whipped my face. I was frozen in my tracks. I hadn't heard him approach at all. He should be more careful. He should have rung his bell. It set my heart racing and I had to take a minute to calm down. I stepped forward again but I'd only walked a few steps when I heard singing. I stopped to listen and for a second there was nothing, but then I could hear it again – lots of little voices wobbling their way around a tune that drifted across the air in front of me so slowly I could almost catch it in a net. It was faint but I could make out the intended melody and it immediately took me back to a school hall with a battered wooden floor, big burgundy curtains and a climbing frame that locked against the wall. I couldn't quite make out the words but it didn't matter because they leapt into my brain as quickly and completely as a fully formed vanishing used to:

Think of a world without any people
Think of a street with no-one living there
Think of a town without any houses
No-one to love and nobody to care.
We thank you, Lord, for families and friendships,
We thank you, Lord, and praise your holy name.

It was my favourite of all the songs we used to sing in school assembly. When Mrs Eccles started playing the opening notes on the piano it always had the same effect on me, a lump would appear in my throat and I would stand with my shoulders back, my chin out and my feet together, just like you were supposed to, ready to sing as well as I could. My eyes hunted out the source of the sound and rested on the back of Gillygate Primary School, about thirty yards away, over scrubby grass, behind a patch of trees. I wandered closer to see if I could get a clearer listen and settled down in the grass, resting against a tree trunk. I must have caught the end of their practice though, because there was only one more chorus to come, and then the piano struck its last high ringing notes and there was only silence and no more singing seeping out into the world for free. My legs weren't for moving me on so I stayed where I was looking onto an empty playground and the school building. The school was red-bricked and old-fashioned-looking – 'Boys' was inscribed in stone in a fussy font over one red door and 'Girls' above another. The schoolyard was sketched out with a caterpillar, numbers running up its wiggly body, a hopscotch grid, and a couple of other designs that were so faded I couldn't tell what they were without getting closer.

After a couple of minutes the 'Boys' red door slowly opened and boys and girls bumbled out into the playground. It was the proper small ones first – ones that looked so tiny and useless you couldn't believe that they'd been let out of the sight of their mums and dads, even for a second. A minute later a lady teacher in a long green skirt pushed through the door and the little ones ran up to her and wrapped their arms around a leg, or grabbed hold of an arm, and she walked around the playground like a slow-moving maypole with kids orbiting her, bumping off one another like dozy bees. Bigger children started pouring out through the other door but they were less interested in the teacher and were off doing the things they normally did at break in a separate part of the yard.

It was obvious within a minute or two of watching which kids were in and which kids were out. I'd clocked two outs within seconds. They were playing together in the corner by a tree. One of the lads had big red hair that grew like a helmet and desperately needed a cut. He had the widest eyes I'd ever seen, like he was permanently startled, like it was always the second after someone had shouted 'BOO!' in his face. The other boy looked like he'd just been released from a prisoner-of-war camp – head shaved and so skinny you feared he would be chilly out, even on a summer's morning. There was nobody else near – just them and a tree in the corner. God knows what they were up to over there, but they appeared oblivious to all the playing going on around them as groups of kids yelled and had fun and shot about one way then the other. These two were huddled together chat, chat, chatting and it was good, I thought, that they had each other at least. At one point a ball bounced over to them, a stray shot from a game going on over the other side of the yard. The lad with the red hair took a wild swing in an attempt to kick it back to the lads who were calling for it, but the ball ended up behind him, to the laughter of the football boys. It took the two of them a further couple of attempts before they managed to send the ball in the intended direction.

I let my eyes move over to the middle, where the

girls congregated and the princesses ruled. Not yet eleven years old and you could already spot them, the two of them, pretty little things, one blonde, one brunette, pristine uniforms and shiny shoes, ponytails bobbing along after them, as were the plainer girls, eager to keep up, to be in on the chat. I could have sat there all day and watched the mucking about and daft games, but a whistle blew and the long process of them all heading back behind the red doors began. The last one finally disappeared, the door banged shut, and the playground was empty again. The sun went behind a cloud, I was back to thinking about the dead little boy in Clifton and I felt so sad that I couldn't move for a few minutes. An old man passed with his dog and gave me a wary look, like I was about to jump up and throttle him with his own lead and kill the dog. I waited until he was long gone so he didn't think he was going to be done over and then I pulled myself up and carried on around the cricket pitch and back home. That night I didn't even try a vanishing; I knew it wouldn't work. I just lay there thinking about those kids, about how small they were, how vulnerable. How easily they would break. It made me shudder to think like that. I hoped someone was keeping an eye on each and every one of them.

5

I've only ever come close to telling one person about what happened in Clifton. Mum always said that it was important to keep the door shut on the past, and over the years she's watched like a hawk to make sure I've done that. She said we were lucky that I was too young to have my name in the paper, and I shouldn't go ruining our fresh start in Raithswaite by talking about things that can never be changed. And I was careful for years until I nearly told Fiona Jackson. I first met her when we were both nine years old, not long after we'd moved to Raithswaite, and she was just the same then as she is now – dark eyes and darker hair. Stern and lovely. The only difference is that seven years later her beauty comes complete with curves. There's an old limestone quarry called Crosshills between our two houses. The back wall of the quarry is sixty feet of vertical rock with trees and grass growing out of it; the bowl below is a maze of tracks, sudden big rocks and tiny steep hills. A few years ago the shrubs and trees began to take over and the place is mainly green now with only the odd patch of grey quarry rock showing through.

I've never made friends easily; all of it is unclear to me and I'm not sure how it normally happens, but with Fiona it happened because of the quarry. She would often be down there avoiding her dad and her brothers, and I would be there too, hiding from Mum on her dark days. It was easier for us to walk around together than to try and pretend the other person wasn't there, and over the years we became easy in each other's company. These days when we meet she's usually got her music and her cigarettes. We sit down if it's sunny, or wander about if it's cold, and she gives me an ear of her headphones, which has got tricky since I grew half a foot in six months, but never offers me a cigarette. I don't want to be misleading – we aren't *best* friends. Sometimes we don't see each other for days, and sometimes we see each other and she might want to be left alone. But most of the time we have a chat and a wander.

It nearly happened because of her brother. He'd just been found guilty of GBH and was starting a two-year sentence. Fiona was angry, but not with the sentence, with her brother. She told me how hard he'd been to live with, how stressed he made her feel and how she was pleased that he was going away. Her hands were shaking and she was pulling on the cigarette too fast and I couldn't work out the right thing to say. But it got worse when she suddenly burst into tears. We were stood at the side of the quarry nearest my house, and she was sobbing and I'd never been alone with a crying girl before. I was useless. I knew I was supposed to hug her, comfort her, but we'd never touched in all the years I'd known her, and I just couldn't move forward and put my arms around her. Gradually she calmed down a little. She was telling me that it was a shit thing to say, but she was relieved when her brother got sentenced, that it meant the house might be normal for a while. 'The thing is, I can't say that to anyone,' she said. 'There's a few people at the house now and it's like a wake. And they are all having a go at the judge and the court, and I'm trying to nod along when all I can see is the truth of what he did, and how I can't stand him and I'm pleased I won't have to live in the same house as him any more.' She looked so sad at that moment, so guilty and tired, like she'd said something she should never say, that I was about to speak too. I was going to tell her about the little boy back in Clifton. I could feel myself running towards the words, charging down the runway. I was excited, I felt relief that I was going to be finally saying it out loud, and Fiona would understand, I knew she would. My mouth was open and I was ready to talk when there was a sharp knocking behind us. We turned to see Mum at the bathroom window, eyes glaring down, gesturing for me to come in. Fiona told me to go, she would be fine she said, and I left her stood there, crying in the quarry. Mum was still in the bathroom, cleaning hard. I asked what she was after, but all she said was 'You'd been out there too long,' and carried on scrubbing at the bath.

That evening we were sat in the back room reading our library books. 'You like that Fiona, don't you?' Mum said, without looking up. I didn't get chance to answer before she carried on. 'It's important Donald, that you don't say anything to her that you shouldn't.' I nodded and said I knew. 'We left all that behind when we left Clifton, so don't go bringing it with you here.' She looked up from her book then and fixed me with a stare. I looked away first. She was like that my mum – if she saw an open drawer she always made sure she snapped it shut.

6

The day after the inset day I headed for the library as usual at dinner, but I could see from the end of the corridor that I wouldn't be spending my time in my usual library spot. Frizzy-haired Emma was sat against the wall in the corridor knitting away and Tom Clarkson was heading down the corridor towards me, his drawing pad underneath his arm, shaking his head. 'Nothing doing Donald, they've got some meeting or something going on and we've been barred.' It didn't matter really; I didn't want to spend a silent hour in the school library. I ended up in the trees on the scruffy grass that looks onto Gillygate Primary School.

The scene was the same as the day before. The football lads tearing around after the ball, the two pretty girls, hand in hand, dancing around, and the youngest ones tumbling about the teacher. The only difference I could see was the lad from the prisoner-of-war camp was stood alone by the tree, muttering away to himself, walking in a circle, rubbing his head, looking lost without his red-haired friend. I watched him for a while, thinking I better not hang around too long, when there were raised voices over the other side of the yard. I could make out two of the football lads rolling around together, taking wide swipes at each other's heads. The whole yard was suddenly running that way, as certain as a tidal wave, everyone seemingly shouting something. The teacher was the fastest of the lot, her brown hair streaking after her as she dashed to the epicentre of the trouble. One of the few people who wasn't engaged in the excitement in some way was the short-haired lad who stayed in the corner with his tree. I moved out of the bushes and over to the railings.

'Hello,' I called. He looked up and around, searching for the mystery voice. I waved my hand and he saw me and waved back. I gestured for him to come over and he trotted up to the railings. His uniform had that second-hand look I could tell a million miles off – frayed collars and cuffs. Faded colours. He looked up at me, his head tipped back so he could get the full view. He shoved a finger towards his manky-looking nose.

'Don't do that.'

He dropped his hand.

'What's your name?'

'Jake.'

'Where's your mate today?'

'Harry?'

'The red-headed lad.'

'Yeah, he's not in today.'

'Why not?'

He shook his bony head and shrugged.

'He's probably sick,' I said.

'Yeah,' he said.

'He's probably hanging over the toilet right now, puking carrots up,' I said.

Jake laughed. 'Yeah, or pooing non-stop!'

'Or both,' I said. 'Sat on the toilet and sicking into a bucket.'

He laughed like a drain at the thought of his friend in such a predicament. His laughing turned into a heavy yawn and he slapped his hand to his forehead and rubbed. I looked over to the other side of the yard. The teacher was getting some control over the situation. She had both lads back on their feet, looking at each other and offering her a series of shrugs. She was encouraging them to shake hands.

'How old are you then Jake?' I asked.

'Eight,' he said.

The lads must have made up then, or at

least pretended to, because the excitement was killed and kids were making their way back over to our side of the yard and resuming their games.

'Well Jake,' I said, 'I'm Donald.'

I put my hand over the railing.

His little hand felt as thin as paper in my big shovel and I made sure I didn't squeeze too hard. We shook.

'See you around,' I said.

'See you around,' he said back.

I glanced over my shoulder as I headed back to Raithswaite High and saw Jake by himself again, over by his tree.

7

We've always been heavy library users. Back in Clifton I won a competition for having borrowed the most books by anyone on a junior ticket over the summer holidays. I was surprised to win; I didn't even know it was a competition they were running. They took a photograph of me with one of the librarians for the local newspaper and gave me a twenty-pound book voucher you could use in any bookshop in the country. It seemed to me a huge amount, but when it came to spending it I couldn't choose, and after we'd been in the shop for half an hour, with me picking up and putting down book after book, Mum snapped and dragged me home. She went back the next day and came home with a dictionary and an atlas. I was disappointed at the time, I really wanted books about spaceships and aliens, but over the years I've used both books many times for homework so I understood her thinking.

Now I go to the library after school. It gives me

more time away from Mum and the house and means I can do homework or research for a new vanishing. That was where I saw Jake next. He was over in the corner on the little plastic chairs with his head in a book.

'All right Jake?'

He looked up at me. His face was grubby and needed a good wipe. He didn't look like he remembered.

'Donald,' I said. 'From the other week.'

'Oh yeah. Hiya Donald.'

'You all right then?' I asked again.

He nodded that he was, and I lowered myself down onto a chair. My knees nearly touched my chin.

'Good to be out of school?' I asked.

'Yeah,' he said.

'It's always good to be out of school isn't it?'

He laughed at that and said, 'Yeah, always good.'

I asked him if he liked school but he didn't seem to know what to say to that so I asked him if he liked books. He knew the answer to that one.

'Horror books, yeah.'

'Is that what you've got there then?'

'Yeah, I've nearly read all of them.'

'Books about dinosaurs?' I asked.

He shrugged. Too old for that now I suppose.

'Books about football?'

He shook his head. Of course not books about football.

'Horror books,' I said.

'Yeah, ghosts and demons and horror and stuff.'

'I like books too. I read loads of books. It's good, isn't it, reading?'

'Sometimes it is,' he said.

'Well, I best get on Jake. See you soon.'

'See you Donald,' he said. It touched me that. To hear my name spoken so friendly.

He was quite often there, over in the kids' corner alone, with his head in a book or sat at one of the computers playing away on a game. Sometimes when his free half-hour ran out I would pay a pound so he could have an extra bit of time. When he was bored he would come and sit with me and we would chat about what he'd been up to. He told me all about his mate, Harry. About how he had all the computer games and how rich his family was and the car his dad drove. He told me about the teachers, the ones he liked and the ones he hated. Sometimes I helped him with homework and other times we both just sat there reading.

It was a Saturday afternoon when I pushed

the library door and it didn't budge. I noticed the sign then: *Library closed due to burst pipe. Sorry for any inconvenience. Post returns through letter box.* I turned to head home and saw Jake shooting up the road towards me, his rucksack banging up and down against his back. He walked fast for a little lad with skinny legs. He saw me as he sped along and gave me a grin and a big wave.

'They're shut Jake,' I said when he reached me.

'Oh,' he said and didn't ask why.

'There's been a burst pipe. They must be flooded,' I told him.

'Right,' he said and nodded.

'Are you off back home then?' I asked.

'I'll go to the playground,' he said, and we set off walking down the road.

It was the one Saturday a year where Raithswaite gets both blue sky and warm sun, and the houses and buildings in town looked smaller than usual, shrunk in the heat, shy with the focus of two bright strangers fixed on them. The roads shimmered hot, people were wearing shorts and T-shirts and I thought that perhaps it was no bad thing that the library was closed, that it was good to be outside on a day like this. We walked ten minutes to the playground, which was just at the end of Jake's street, and wasn't much of a playground at all. It was a scruffy place, tucked away at the far end of Fox Street, and there was nobody about, not even on a bright Saturday.

We had a go on the swings and the climbing frame and mucked around for a while before Jake got bored.

'Have you got some of your books in that bag?' I asked him, and he nodded that he did.

'Why don't we have a read of one of your horror stories then?' I said.

He pulled a book out of his bag, held it up and said, 'I was taking it back. It's rubbish. It's not even scary.'

'The scarier the better?' I asked.

'Yeah,' said Jake, and I hit on a plan.

'That book might not be scary in the sun in the middle of the day. It might be scary if you read it in a haunted house.'

'A haunted house?' he said.

'Have you ever been to one?'

Jake shook his head. 'Somebody said the toilets at school are haunted but I don't believe them.'

'Do you want to see a haunted house?'

He squinted his eyes up towards me.

'Do you know where there is one?'

I told him that I did.

43

We left the playground; he was so excited, walking ahead, that I had to grab his collar to pull him slower.

I hadn't invented the house; there is a house somewhere in Raithswaite that's said to be haunted, a house where a tragedy occurred, it's just that I've never been quite sure exactly where it is. But I knew of an abandoned house that looked like it *should* be haunted, a house that if someone told you it *was* haunted, you would think they were telling you the truth. The place I had in mind was the old quarry house, a wreck at the south side of the quarry, about half a mile from my house. It's next to the old entrance where the trucks used to drive in and out, and it's been empty ever since we moved to Raithswaite. It sits back from the road, nestled under tall trees. Every year it slips closer to ruin, and on dark nights when the mist comes down from the hills and there's frost in the air, it can make you shudder to see it so abandoned and ruined. The quarry master used to live there, the man who logged the loads of the trucks and looked after the quarry in the night, making sure people weren't stealing any rock. When the quarry closed he lost his job and moved out of the house and nobody has lived there since. That was my haunted house for Jake and I hoped that it didn't look too friendly in the sun.

44

I told Jake the story of the real haunted house as we walked along. It's a story that's passed along from year to year at the high school and all the older kids in Raithswaite know it. I told him that it started when Mr Lorriemore was getting his gear together to go hunting. He was downstairs, it was about half five in the morning, and he'd filled his flask and packed his bag and was checking that everything was in working order with his rifle. Just as he was aiming it skyward his wife was climbing out of bed to make sure that he hadn't forgotten to pack the sandwiches she'd made for him. She left the bed, stood and reached for her dressing gown, and was about to make her way across the room when Mr Lorriemore took a pretend potshot. He pulled the trigger, but there was a bullet in the chamber that shouldn't have been there, and the bullet went straight through the floorboards and into his wife. She fell to the floor and was dead in minutes. It's said that when the ambulance and police turned up Mr Lorriemore was hugging his dead wife's body, weeping. Mrs Lorriemore was carried out of the house, covered in a blanket, and Mr Lorriemore was arrested and led away. There was lots of gossip at the time about another man and revenge on Mr Lorriemore's part, but when the police came and took measurements and did their investigation, everything confirmed the story Mr Lorriemore had told them. There was a hole in the ceiling and the bullet had entered Margaret Lorriemore at such an angle that it had to have come from below. The police concluded that a man intent on taking revenge on a cheating wife would not take a potshot through floorboards and be lucky to strike gold with his first and only shot. Mr Lorriemore eventually left Raithswaite and was never seen again. I told Jake that some said it was guilt that drove him from town, but the more popular story was that he couldn't bear to stay in the house and hear his wife's ghost calling out the name of another man.

'So he shot her dead?' Jake asked.

'He did.'

'And she's the ghost?'

'She is.'

'And that's where we're going?'

'It is.'

He started to speed up again.

It had been years since I'd been to the house. It sits at the furthest point in the quarry away from my house, but I knew that the best way in was still probably through the back door that had been forced open years ago. We stopped at the front gate, both of us hot from the walk in the sun, and rested for a second.

'Do you still want to go in?' I asked. Jake nodded, I opened the gate and we walked up the path and around the back.

'You OK?' I asked Jake as we stood looking at the house.

'Is this it then? Is this the haunted house?' he wanted to know. I told him it was and he looked at it like he believed me. I followed his eyes and could see that the look of the place would convince any eight-year-old it was haunted. It must have been white back in the glory days of the quarry, but now it stood grey and desolate, broken and sad-looking. Even in the sun on a Saturday afternoon I could almost believe that it was haunted myself.

'Shall we go in then?' he asked.

'Are you sure?' I knew he was sure but I wanted to build the tension.

'Yeah, let's go in, but you go first.'

We approached the door and I gave it a hard shove with my shoulder and pushed until it opened. I walked a few steps into the cool dark and waited. I turned to the light of the half-open door and saw that Jake's confidence had evaporated. He was stood just inside the door, a small black silhouette against the sunny day, one quick step away from daylight and overgrown greenery.

'You don't have to come any further, you know.' I didn't want to make him do anything he didn't want to do.

'No,' he said, 'I want to.' But he didn't make a move forward.

'We could just sit in the garden and read the books and look at the house,' I told him.

'I want to come in though,' he said, but his body betrayed him and he stayed rooted to the spot like a tree stump.

'Do you want to hold my hand?' I asked. He nodded. I went back and took his hand and said, 'If you get scared just tell me, and we'll leave straight away.' He nodded again and we slowly stepped forward down the hallway. He giggled with excitement.

'Have you seen her? The *ghost*?'

He whispered the word, like the mention of it might provoke an appearance.

'I haven't, no. I haven't seen her, but I have heard her,' I told him.

'What does she sound like?'

He held my hand tighter in anticipation of the answer. I could feel the blood thrumming quickly around his warm fingers. He stepped closer to hear my answer.

'She sounds like she's dying,' I said. 'I live over at the far side of the quarry and sometimes at night you can hear her wailing. On still nights it echoes and carries and sounds like wolves. Over the years people who don't know the story have rung the police but the police have stopped coming because they've never found anything.'

'Maybe they've stopped coming because they're scared,' said Jake.

He was so close now he was almost under my feet. I sensed he was keener and more scared at the same time. We'd either be going right into the house or running back out into the garden and I couldn't tell which.

'Well, they do say that policemen who have caught all kinds of criminals and seen dead bodies smashed up in road accidents won't come back in here after they've been in once.'

'Really? Let's go a bit further.'

I had to stifle a laugh at that. We reached a doorway on the left and looked in and saw a shell of a room. It was brighter in there; the sun was strong enough to cut through the thick garden shrubs and the cracked and dirty windows and the light made Jake braver. He let go of my hand and walked in.

'Was this the room he shot her from?' he asked. I looked up at the ceiling and saw there were enough cracks and scuffs there for it to seem plausible.

'I think so,' I said. 'Can you see that mark on the ceiling there? That looks like it could have been done by a bullet.'

Jake grinned as he peered up. He was more excited than scared now and was keen to see the rest of the house. We wandered around downstairs and found most of the rooms to be as bare as the first room. In what must have been the kitchen there were still some cupboards on the wall, and a sink, but other than that, nothing.

'Do you think there are rats?' Jake asked. I told him of course there were rats, and he was almost as pleased by this as the thought of the shooting and the ghost. We went upstairs next and he wanted to hold hands again, but I told him I would have to go first to check that the floorboards would take our weight. I creaked my way slowly up the stairs and then shouted for Jake to follow me. There were three bedrooms, all empty, and a wreck of a bath-room. The wallpaper was still clinging on desper-ately in patches in some rooms, as if the structure of the house depended on it. One strong shoulder charge at any of the walls and I was sure I could bring the whole place down. We sat down in the room where I told Jake Mrs Lorriemore had ended up dead. We rested against a wall and listened to see if we could hear anything ghostlike. When there was nothing that we could even pretend might be a ghost I grabbed his shoulder and said, 'Jake. What was that?'

'What?' he asked, and leant forward to listen.

'That!'

'There isn't anything,' he said, and I turned quickly and shouted a big 'BOO!' at him. He screamed so loudly the noise ran into every room in the house and hung in the air, but he almost immediately started laughing, and he'd enjoyed it, I could tell. We sat there for a while and it didn't seem like the time to be reading the books, and Jake was more interested in the story of the haunted house than the ghost story in his bag anyway. After half an hour of chatting and making more stuff up I told him we should get him home. As we were walking down the stairs I said, 'It's a pity we won't be here tonight Jake, that's when she'll come out and start with her wailing.'

'You think she'll be here tonight?' he asked.

'Saturday nights she's always about and she's always the loudest then,' I told him. 'Saturday nights her husband met his friends in town and they drank till they were silly, so she always took the opportunity to meet the other man. She cries the loudest on Saturday nights.'

'Maybe we should come back tonight then,' he said, and I had to laugh at that. Even I didn't want to be creeping around the quarry house in the dark. We walked back in the direction of his house, his pace not as fast now there were no haunted houses at the end of the walk.

'Do you not go out anywhere on Saturday afternoons Jake?' I asked him.

He shook his head.

'Won't your mum have noticed you've been gone so long?'

'Steve comes round and they like to be alone, so I have to play out till teatime. Can we go back to the haunted house?'

'Next Saturday?'

He nodded.

'We can if you want.'

'Maybe we'll see her next week,' he said.

We agreed to meet at the playground and I walked him back to the end of Fox Road, and stood and watched until he walked through his front door.

There was nothing left for me to do other than go home and I set off feeling flat after the fun we'd had that afternoon. All I had to look forward to for the rest of the day was Mum and her moods. I walked up our street, the house came into view and I slowed – I could sniff trouble on the air. Sometimes just by looking at our house you can see that you'll be walking into a fight. I stopped fifty yards off and had a think. I thought about not going in at all, but I knew that was just kicking trouble and running away when you had to come back down the same road later. The sooner it's done the better, like throwing up – get it out of the way, clean your teeth and move on. I shut the front door behind me, careful not to be too quiet like I was sneaking, careful not to slam and set her on edge. Noise was coming from the kitchen and I followed the sound. She was at the sink, shoulders up round her ears, scrubbing at a pan like it was a bad dog that'd rolled in muck. She didn't turn round.

'You've got a fine. For a book about fishing communities in Scotland or some nonsense. They say it's important you bring it back, they got it you from Oxford or somewhere and they need to send it back now.'

She carried on rubbing that pan raw and I saw the letter and the torn envelope on the kitchen table.

'They shouldn't bother with your silly requests.'

As I watched her tight back, her strong arms, jutting in and out, rubbing away, words came into my head and I told myself not to risk it. I told myself to run up to my bedroom and everything would be fine.

'You shouldn't open my mail. It's illegal to open somebody else's mail.'

That did it. She spun round and was upon me. Suds were flying as she waved her white candyfloss arms in the air. Her eyes were bright and clear with the certainty of the mad. She ranted about a mother's eternal right to know every thought and action of any child she bore.

'Particularly with you Donald, though, yes? With what you've put this family through? You can't blame me at all for wanting to know the details of what *you've* been up to, can you?' I started edging my way to the door and towards the sanctuary of my bedroom. I already wished I hadn't provoked her. I didn't want hysterics and anger. I wanted to be safe and quiet in my bedroom, thinking about the fun I'd had with Jake at the haunted house. That was all.

8

Kindness is important. I learnt that at an early age
and I've always tried to keep it in mind. The first
real act of kindness I remember was back in Clifton
when I was eight years old, a few months before the
trouble. Things were still good then and I remember being a happy little boy. Happy except for Wednesday nights and Thursday mornings. Wednesday
nights I cried myself to sleep because Thursday
morning was swimming. We'd started lessons that
year and everyone else in the class was excited, piling
onto the coach like we were on our way to a party,
but they all had nothing to fear because they could
swim already. I'd only just learnt to ride a bike, had
never been near a swimming pool in my life and had
to make a special trip to buy a pair of trunks for the
first lesson of term. Six weeks into the term I was
the only kid still in the shallow end, Mr Bowering,
our teacher from school, watching over me as I refused to do anything that involved putting my head

under water. I could see the rest of the class splashing around in the deep water, not a care in the world, and I wondered how they were all so brave. I didn't tell anyone how scared I was, I couldn't articulate the terror, but on Wednesday nights I imagined myself drowning over and over again, the water covering my head, rushing up my nose, flooding through my ears, filling my insides, making me heavy until I sank like a dying ship. Every week I was afraid that I would be made to join the others in the deep end and I was sure that there, amongst all the splashing and noise and confusion, I would sink to the bottom and drown without anyone noticing.

We would come out of the dressing room and line up, waiting for instructions, a row of nearly naked primary school kids, all shapes and sizes, the water shimmering in front of us, silent and menacing, as terrifying as a shark. Mrs Hesketh, the swimming instructor, would be there already waiting to tell us the activity for the week, and it was always something that confirmed my fear, something that involved your head going under the water. But every week, when she was splitting us into groups, Mr Bowering would quietly steal me away and walk me to the shallow end, and I'd be so relieved tears would prickle my eyes. Each week he would try and help me along, try and get me more confident, but each week I became more scared and he would let me out of the pool and into the changing rooms earlier and earlier. He never became impatient, never lost his temper. At some point he must have spoken to my mum because after one lesson he came to find me in the empty changing rooms. He sat with me and told me that I was to wait for him outside the staff room after school, that we were coming back to the pool. 'We're going to crack this phobia, me and you,' he said, patting me on the shoulder. 'Swimming is supposed to be fun.'

After the last lesson of the day, terrified, feeling like I was on death row, I waited outside the brown staff room door for him. He drove me to the pool, paid us in and came into the changing rooms with me. But this time, instead of coming out from his cubicle in shorts, T-shirt and flip-flops, he appeared in nothing but a pair of blue trunks. He was a big, curly-haired man, and the thick dark curls on his head covered his arms and chest too. Hair on his front ran in a heavy dark line up from his trunks, over his belly, spreading out like a pair of hairy wings across his chest. As he walked ahead of me I noticed two patches of finer hair on his back, one above, one below his shoulder blades; like little pads of hair sewn into the skin. It was strange to see a teacher so naked, and I didn't know where to put my eyes, but I made sure I didn't stare at the heavy bulge that strained the front of his trunks, pushing them out in a way that didn't happen with any of the lads in my class.

There was hardly anyone else in the pool that afternoon, just a couple of old people swimming breaststroke slowly up and down the far lane. When Mr Bowering started to climb down the steps into the deep end, my panic increased. I eyed the safe, shallow water desperately, but he caught me looking and said, 'Not today Donald. Today we make progress.' *This is it, this is when I drown*, I thought. *Clifton Baths, 4.30, Thursday afternoon.* Once he was in the pool he let himself sink down and stayed under for a few seconds before he erupted out of the water. He pulled himself to the side and shook the water clear from his head. 'See Donald, it's easy.' I wanted nothing to do with it.

Climbing into the deep end felt like climbing into death, but as soon as the water reached my chest I sensed Mr Bowering behind me, ready to hold me up if needed. Still, I clung to the side of the pool until my fingers hurt. We started slowly with treading water and when I had mastered that we moved on to doggy paddling. I wasn't happy with any of it, but with Mr Bowering in the water next to me I felt less convinced I was about to drown, and slowly I started to make progress. Each week he pushed me more than I was happy to be pushed, but with each session I grew in confidence. For six weeks he taught me outside of school time and by the end of the sixth week I was swimming widths in the deep end, happy to jump into the pool and let the water swallow me whole. In one lesson, in front of the whole class, Mr Bowering asked me to dive into the deep end from the diving board. When I broke the surface the whole class cheered, it was like I was a star in a film, and best of all, my fear had dissolved. That was how I learnt about kindness. I learnt that sometimes it's important to give yourself and your time to someone, that it really can make a difference to someone's life if you make the effort.

*

I didn't see Jake during the week. Mum got it into her head that the backyard needed an overhaul and I had to be on hand to dig up paving stones, empty the wheelbarrow, creosote the fence and spring-clean the shed. She wanted me home straight after school and to refuse would be more bother than keeping quiet and getting it done. I didn't mind much anyway. Hard work stopped me from thinking too much, wore me out and helped me sleep. But by the time Saturday came round again I was looking forward to seeing him. I woke up almost happy, pleased to have something to look forward to, and I set off to the playground a good half an hour before I expected to see him. But I didn't see him at all. Two hours I sat there. And it wasn't the weather for it like it had been the week before, all sunny and gentle. The wind had an edge that aimed itself at my neck and the threat of rain was never far away. There I was, sat on a bench in a playground, at the wrong side of town, with a bag full of little boys' ghost stories I'd picked from the library shelves. I felt stupid. When I realised that he wasn't about to turn up I walked up and down Fox Street a couple of times and glanced at the house, but there was nothing to tell me whether anyone was home or not. Then I was struck by another thought. Maybe he'd forgotten what we'd said and gone straight to the haunted house. I headed over there right away but the place was deserted, no sign of anyone at all. When I finally gave up and trudged home I stopped being annoyed and started to worry. What if something had happened? He could have been flattened by one of the massive Raithswaite

Chemical lorries that roar through the town faster than they should. He could have had a row with his mum and run off and been picked up by a pervert. I thought of all the terrible trouble he could be in and got myself into a state. It's something that's happened since Clifton and the little boy. I can't control my thinking and it runs away with itself and I manage to convince myself that terrible tragedies are happening everywhere and nothing can be done to stop any of them. And even though I know I'm being irrational, I can't control it, I can't drag myself away from the thoughts. By the end of Sunday I'd had him dead six different times in six different ways.

As soon as the lunch bell sounded on Monday I was up and off, straight to Gillygate Primary. I could tell from halfway round the cricket pitch that my weekend concern had been misplaced. There were two familiar figures over in the corner by the tree and as I got closer it became clear that one was bright-haired Harry, the other skinny Jake. It was a warm blanket of relief to see him there. I didn't go close; I hung back, just near enough to check that everything was fine. I watched them for a couple of minutes and then a whistle blew and they all charged towards the red doors.

The next Saturday at the library he came over to me as happy as Larry. 'Hi Donald.'

I put my book down.

'You all right Jake?'

He nodded that he was.

'Where were you last Saturday?'

He racked his brains. He dragged the memory back from somewhere.

'Harry's.'

'I thought we were going to the haunted house?'

'I had to go to Harry's.'

'Did you have a good time?'

He shook his head.

'His house smells funny and his mum made pasta.'

'Don't you like pasta?'

'Makes me puke.'

He bent over and did an impression of someone throwing up their tea. He stopped mid-gag when something more pressing entered his head.

'Shall we go to the haunted house now?' he asked.

'Is that what you want to do? We can do something else.'

But it was definitely the haunted house he was after. He took his new books up to the counter to get them stamped and we set off. On the way we stopped at a corner shop and I bought us a couple of cans and some chocolate for a treat.

After a brief wander looking for ghosts and rats we ended up in the room where Mrs Lorriemore was shot dead. I told him the best place to read a ghost story was in a haunted house and I handed him one of the books, but he wanted me to read, so we sat down against the wall, he chose which book he wanted to hear and I started. When he'd finished with his drink and chocolate he moved himself closer so he could follow the words as I read. After a page or two he dropped his head against my arm and it was good to have his warm body tucked next to mine, comfortable and relaxed. I read the stories to him as best I could. I tried out some voices and he didn't laugh at my attempts and he huddled in close. After we'd worked through a couple of the books he wanted to know if I'd heard the ghost woman and her wailing since the last time we were at the house together.

'That very night,' I told him. He pulled himself away at this news and looked to me for more information.

'Do you remember that it was a warm day? Well that night I went to bed with the window open to let in some air, but I had to shut it because the wailing was so bad. The worst I've ever heard.'

'Like wolves?' he said.

'Like starving wolves,' I told him.

'And the police didn't dare come?'

'Nobody left their houses.'

'But we're here now and we aren't scared.'

'We must be braver than most.'

'Yeah, they're all a bunch of chickens,' he said and flapped his arms and shook his head. He carried on this way for a while. What a great little lad. I got him to choose another story after he'd quietened down and we raced through that one before heading back outside.

We mucked about in the garden for a while before I took him home. Or rather Jake mucked around and I supervised. He was chasing about, pretending to be an aeroplane, making all sorts of engine noises and having a good time. I was keeping a close eye on him, aware of the danger posed by the pond in the far corner, but he surprised me – it wasn't the pond he went for, it was the tall tree in the opposite corner. He clocked it on one of his sweeps of the garden. He stopped by the trunk and looked up at the branches with his hands on his hips. Before I had chance to warn him he'd swung and scrambled his way up into the lower branches. I ran from the far side of the garden and shouted at him to be careful, to come down, but he was having too much fun up there to listen to me. I didn't like it at all – him up there at risk and me not being able to do anything. I thought about climbing the tree myself, to try and get him to come down, but I could see that might cause him to lose concentration and fall. Eventually I managed to talk him down, but it took a while. When I got him back to ground level I crouched down and held his shoulders and looked into his eyes and tried to explain how dangerous it was, what he'd done, how he needed to be more careful, but he could only hear nagging and didn't understand the truth of my words.

'I climb all the time,' he said. 'I like it.'

'You wouldn't like it if you fell and smashed your back up and couldn't move from the neck down, would you?' I said. But he was charging off before I got to the end of the sentence, an aeroplane again, dive-bombing imaginary towns. It's true what they say, you have to watch them every second. They're drawn to danger.

9

I haven't seen anyone since we left Clifton. No therapists, psychotherapists, or counsellors. There was no legal requirement and Mum thought it better not to dwell on any of it. 'They've done tests Donald. On soldiers back from war who saw and did terrible things. Those that went to see head doctors and talked about it and relived it over and over recovered more slowly than those that kept shut and got on with things.' So that was that. As far as she was concerned the second we closed the door of the new house in Raithswaite it was finished with. Outside of the house was a town where nobody knew about it, inside the house it wouldn't be mentioned. We only ever spoke about that day once, and not even properly then. It was after the last police interview. She sat me down at the kitchen table and looked at me and said,

'Donald. Was there anything you could have done to stop it? The accident?'

I stalled for time. 'I shouldn't have gone past number sixty-five,' I said.

'No, I don't mean that. Was there anything you could have done to stop it from happening when you were down there?'

I shook my head.

'Tell me,' she said. 'Go through it one more time for me. And it's just you and me now, you won't get into trouble.'

So I told it again. The same as I'd told it at the police station. How I was riding my bike and I didn't see him until it was too late, when he was suddenly there in front of me. She interrupted.

'What do you mean "suddenly"? There was *nothing* you could do?' she asked. She was staring at me as if she might never blink again. I stuck with what I'd said at the police station. 'I didn't know what had happened until I got up and saw him,' I told her. She took a deep breath and rocked her head from left to right as if she was shaking any doubts away for good.

'Right,' she said. 'Bad things happen all the time to people all over the world. There have been thousands before you and there will be thousands after. The best thing you can do is to pick yourself up, dust yourself down and get on with things.'

She looked at me again. 'As for that little lad and his mother . . .'

I waited for what she was going to say about the little boy and his mum, I'd been waiting for weeks, but the words never came. After a long silence she shook her head and hugged her cup. That was her final comment on the matter. Sometimes she looked worried that I was even *thinking* about it. She would squint at me when I'd been quiet for a while, as if to say, *You better not be thinking those kind of thoughts in this house Donald.*

For a while being in a new town helped. The fact that I was trying to settle kept me busy. And there was Mum and her moods to duck and hide from. But it never went away. I don't see how it ever could. I tried to control my thinking. If something came on TV that brought back memories I turned the TV off. If I saw something that reminded me when I was out and about I looked away or walked off in the other direction. When any discussion in a lesson brought back a memory I stopped listening, regardless of whether it would get me into trouble. But it didn't work. You can't stop thinking about something just because you want to.

Close your eyes.

Empty your head of all of its thoughts.

Don't picture a clown.

So I've been thinking about it for years. My brain is drawn to that morning and its consequences over and over and I can't leave it alone, like wasps and jam. My fingers work at the itch until the skin gives way and then I keep scratching deeper. The panic has grown along with my comprehension. When I was eight I understood it to be a bad thing like I understood lying, hitting and kicking, and war to be bad things. Kindness, sharing and caring were good things. That was my moral compass. Back then I didn't realise what it *meant* to have killed someone. That every second I was alive he wasn't. That every time I looked at the sky, stroked a dog, ate a cake, ran a race, drank a drink, read a book, went to sleep, cleaned my teeth, combed my hair, woke up, sat down, stood up, he couldn't. And all the things he couldn't do, his mum and dad were there to see him not doing them. I didn't understand back then that every moment I was alive he was dead. I didn't understand that he could never do anything ever again.

It took a while after it happened before I started thinking thoughts like that. There was no terror at first, not like there is now. I was upset back then, but the real truth of it has crept up over the years. On a good day I can convince myself that I was involved in a terrible accident where someone ended up dead and there was nothing I could have done about it. I can breathe on those days. On a bad day the only thought in my head is: *I killed a little boy.* On a bad day breathing is shallow, there's not enough oxygen in the air and there's not enough air in a whole sky for my lungs. I see risk everywhere. Every time someone gets in a car, every time someone crosses a road. Every time someone mentions they have a headache. I see and hear those things and expect they are going to end in disaster. I'm surprised when I leave the house and return safely in the evening. I'm surprised to see that Mum has made it through the day too. Frankly, it's a hundred tiny shocks to me that anyone makes it through a whole day. During a bad period every part of my body and brain is only made of guilt. Hands, arms, feet, legs, blood, bones – all cast-iron guilt. Heavy, black and dragging. They had a book on display in the library a few months ago: *Guilt and How It Gets in the Way.* I took it down from the shelf and went for a read in a quiet corner. There was a chapter on what guilt is, a chapter on self-esteem, a chapter on enforcing boundaries, a chapter on reclaiming your life. As I flicked through it, it dawned on me that it was a book for people who had no reason to feel guilt at all. It was a book for stupid people. There were no chapters on what you should do if you'd killed someone and guilt was pulling you to the ground. I was angry. For the few seconds I carried the book from the display to my chair I felt the sharp ache of hope. I thought there might be something in those pages that could help. Something that would absolve me. I dropped the book to the floor and kicked it under a shelf and went home and cried. On a bad day it's like I'm filling with water from the inside and there's nothing anyone can do, not even Mr Bowering, to stop me from drowning.

And then there was hell to consider. I looked into hell. I had to. There can't be too many things you would end up in hell for, but killing a two-year-old must be on the list. I researched it at the library. I'd been feeling sick about it for weeks so I thought it might be better to get a look at where I was heading. I told the lady who was helping me find the books that it was for a school project. 'It's a bit gruesome,' she said, 'I think you drew the short straw. Next time try and get heaven.'

She gathered a few books together and I took them to the reference room and started to read. I didn't understand some of the passages at all, but there were lots of pictures of flames and burning men and the devil. I read in one book that hell was eternal damnation, that it was always burning away and always hot. Another book said that some people believed hell to be cold and gloomy, and one said that Earth itself and here and now was hell. That one made some sense to me. But if scholars couldn't decide what hell even *was*, how was I to know what to expect? I saw the librarian who'd helped me putting books back onto shelves. I pushed my books to one side and went over to her.

'Do you believe in hell?' I asked.

She stopped what she was doing, put a big book down on a table. She straightened herself and held her hands together and stared off into space. After a few seconds she glanced around to see if anyone was near, and leant in close to me and said, 'No. No I don't. I think it's all mumbo-jumbo.'

She smelt nice. She smelt of hope.

'Thanks,' I told her.

'But don't put that in your project,' she said.

I left the library with that thought in my head. Mumbo-jumbo. Hell was mumbo-jumbo. And that from a woman who must have read a lot of books. It was something to cling on to.

But the terror of it never goes away. You can go for days thinking that you're doing well, but all you're doing is holding the panic at bay for a while, and that feeling of terror and horror is something that is only ever one thought away. The only thing I can compare it to is a feeling I had back when I was about six years old, back before I'd done anything wrong. It was a summer night and still light and warm outside but I'd been put to bed. My window was open and I could hear older children playing a game of football out in the street, neighbours were in their gardens, chatting to each other. Even my mum was down there. I wasn't tired at all and wanted to be with everyone having fun. I tossed and turned and grumbled to myself. I was thirsty. I went down to ask if I could have a drink and maybe a snack too. The front door was shut, which was unusual; when Mum was out at the front she normally left it open. I opened the door onto a silver-grey and silent world. I walked out into the street and looked up and down, but there was nobody there. All the houses were sat back in the shadows, no lights on anywhere. The world had ended and I was six years old and terrified. I started running up and banging on neighbours' doors, shouting and yelling. Where was everyone? I was halfway up the street when I heard Mum shouting for me. I turned and saw her running towards me in her nightie. I ran as fast as I could, back towards her.

She grabbed hold of me. 'Good God Donald, what on earth are you doing? Why are you waking the street up?'

'I heard you all talking and I wanted a drink so I came downstairs.'

'It's one o'clock in the morning.'

'I heard everyone out in the street.'

'That was five hours ago! You've been asleep for five hours.'

I was confused. I couldn't have been asleep. I didn't remember falling asleep. I remembered that I didn't feel tired at all.

A few of the neighbours' bedroom lights were on now and they were looking down onto us as Mum dragged me back to our house, waving sorry to everyone, and pointing a finger at me, shrugging her shoulders. I was still frightened and confused but no longer terrified. But that moment when I walked out into the deserted street, when I thought the world had ended and I was left alone at six years old in the dark, the terror I felt then is the same feeling that has always been there since the day of the trouble. It's not always right in front of me, jumping up and down. Sometimes it is, but even when it's not, it's lurking, it's on my back. What makes it worse is that there isn't anything anyone can do to make it better. Mum running down the street to me in the middle of the night can't make this terror disappear.

10

We didn't move just because I was caught in the garden and because Mum was scared of bumping into the boy's parents. There were problems with older lads too. The first time it happened was just a few days after the trouble. There was a knock at the door early one evening and when Mum answered it I heard a voice I didn't recognise. Nothing seemed too unusual until our door was quickly slammed shut and Mum came into the back room and told me to get upstairs. Her voice sounded like stone being shredded and I quickly did as I was told. It was a summer night and my bedroom window was open and I could hear people out on the street. After a couple of minutes lying on my bed listening to the voices and wondering what was happening I walked over to the window and looked out. I could see a group of what seemed to me men, although they were probably only lads the age that I am now, and they were on the pavement in front of our house.

They looked like they were having fun – a group chatting in the evening heat, a couple of them on bikes, some holding cans at their side. They didn't seem like trouble to me and I wondered what had been said to Mum to make her slam the door and turn her voice so strange. Then one of them looked up at the window and clocked me. He pointed without saying a word, and they all turned and looked. It was a strange reaction they had. There was a cheer, some pretend gasps and the odd word shouted. One of them threw an empty can, but it didn't get close and ended up in next door's hedge. Mum must have been as fast to the phone as I was upstairs because a police car drove down the road then and the lads scattered, discarding more cans as they went. After the police had gone and I was allowed back downstairs I asked Mum what had been said when she opened the door, but she wouldn't tell me. She shook her head and said it was just a lot of silly boys and tried to raise a smile. But then they came back the next night. Mum knew not to answer the door this time, she sent me upstairs again and made sure I went to her bedroom at the back. I could still hear them, faintly, out at the front, shouting to each other, maybe shouting to me, I couldn't tell. They came back regularly, but because they didn't

throw anything again or do anything illegal the police stopped answering Mum's calls. Mum grew
quieter and thinner with the stress of it. Her cheeks
hollowed out, the patches under her eyes darkened,
and her breath started to smell. One Friday night,
just as I was falling asleep, I heard hissing below me
down in the front garden. In my sleepiness I imagined a massive snake sliding around down there,
but then I heard giggling and I knew the naughty
lads were back. I thought about going to tell Mum,
but if they were just pretending to be snakes in our
front garden, well, that was better than knocking on
the front door and making her cry, so I left them to
it. The next morning we got ready to go into town.
When Mum turned to lock the door she froze with
the key in mid-air. I was stood behind her and had
to step to the side to see what was causing the delay.
Someone had sprayed 'Psycho Killer!' in red paint
across the front door. The key never made it into the
lock. Mum grabbed me by the shoulder, pushed me
back inside and slammed the front door shut behind
us. She went straight up to her room. I did the same
and we lay in silence in our bedrooms. Or maybe she
was crying quietly, she had been doing that quite often. Lying there, it took me a minute before I realised
that I was the psycho killer the paint was referring to.

It was when Mr Mole turned up that I realised we wouldn't be staying in Clifton much longer. Even before the trouble Mum wasn't the friendliest of people and we didn't have neighbours calling round all the time, but we both liked Mr Mole and he seemed to like us back, despite Mum's reserve. He came to see us a few days after the accident and then he arrived a couple of days after the graffiti was sprayed. Mr Mole was one of the neighbours Mum would leave me with and I'd spent lots of days at his house, reading and playing, as he sat with his newspaper, or did the washing up, or mowed his lawn. I liked Mr Mole, he was my favourite of the neighbours to be left with, and we always went to him first. But occasionally he would be away, or he wouldn't be well, and I would have to go elsewhere. Those were always long and awkward days. Mrs Armer would insist I helped her with her baking and cleaning and would try to teach me how to knit. Mr and Mrs Seedall had never had children and watched me like I was an animal in a zoo, like I might suddenly turn wild and decide to break everything I could get my hands on. At the Seedalls' you weren't allowed to watch TV and at three o'clock every afternoon Mrs Seedall went upstairs for her afternoon nap and everything had to be even more silent than it had been all morning.

Mr Seedall had no idea what to do with me for that hour, but he must have been given instructions not to let me out of his sight, so we sat in the front room, both pretending to read, and time did long division on itself until one hour felt like ten. In some ways the stillness at their house prepared me for life with Mum after the trouble.

But Mr Mole was easy to stay with. He didn't care what I did or didn't do. I could go anywhere in his house and he didn't follow. I could turn the TV on and off whenever I wanted and watch anything I liked. If he was working in the garden, or decorating a room, I could help or sit on the couch and read my books and let him get on with it. I did have to take his dog, Scruffy, for a walk with him every afternoon, but he always let me hold the lead and I enjoyed that anyway. When Mum wasn't well once, and had to go and stay with Aunty Sandra to be looked after, I stayed with Mr Mole for a couple of weeks because it was term time and I couldn't miss that much school. It was a brilliant two weeks. We had fish and chips from the chippy, he let me have shandy when he had his drinks in the evening, and he let me stay up later than Mum did. I watched programmes with him Mum would never let me watch. And I don't think it was just me who was sad when it was over. 'We've had a good time together, haven't we Donald?' he said, when Mum turned up and I had to go and pack my stuff. 'He's been good company.'

When he turned up after the graffiti was sprayed he brought with him a box of vegetables from his garden. He spoke more loudly and cheerfully than he usually did. I followed him and Mum into the kitchen and answered Mr Mole's questions and wondered when Mum was going to start speaking. But she didn't speak at all. She looked at the box on the kitchen table as if it contained dead puppies, not potatoes and cabbage, and I thought she might burst into tears. When it became clear that Mum wasn't going to speak Mr Mole rubbed his head a lot and kept saying, 'Well then, well then.' He didn't stay long and I knew then that we wouldn't be in Clifton much longer. The dead little boy, my midnight garden visit and the bunch of bad lads had all combined to make Clifton impossible in Mum's eyes. Mr Mole could be as kind as he liked but nothing was going to keep us there.

11

I'd been sneaking out of school and watching the kids at Gillygate Primary more. There's so much life to them, so much spirit, that the thought of sitting in a near-empty school library just can't compare. It cheers me up to see them all enjoying themselves, to see them charging around, having fun, falling out, falling over. Mainly I go to check that Jake is safe and sound, but it's good to watch the others too. I have my favourites and I make sure they are all there and that all appears well. I make mental notes of faces and characteristics so I can quiz Jake and see what he has to say about them.

I was down there the other day and it was worrying to see Jake alone by the tree. He'd been alone when Harry was at home sick, but this time, after a quick glance around, I could see Harry over the other side of the yard with the football lads, trying to join in their game. He was rubbish, useless, but they were letting him play. And I couldn't help noticing that he'd gone through a bit of a transformation. His hair had been trimmed down and thinned out, it was all up in spikes and he was wearing a new jacket. It was hard to tell from a distance but it looked like he had new trainers too. He looked good. I wanted to go over and chat with Jake and make sure he was OK, but there were two teachers in the yard and there was never an opportunity to get close enough without being spotted. I only went back one more day that week but the scene was the same: useless Harry being tolerated by the football lads, Jake alone by the tree.

'We fell out,' Jake said, on the Saturday. It was clear he was sad – there was none of the speed that normally comes with him and he hardly said a word. He didn't start to open up until we were settled in the upstairs room at the haunted house.

'He said my breath stank.'

'Well it doesn't,' I told him.

'It doesn't does it not?'

He looked up at me with a face full of hope.

'Not even the slightest,' I told him. 'People always say things that are untrue in arguments.'

'But he said I always smelt and my clothes were rubbish.'

'Well I'd try not to worry about it Jake. It doesn't

matter about clothes, does it? Look, my clothes are rubbish too and I'm doing all right.'

Jake looked me over but didn't say anything.

'Is there anyone else you could be friendly with?' I asked.

He started to cry then. A flood of little boy's tears poured from him. Snot bubbles formed and popped and formed again. His shoulders shook. There was nothing to do but hold him until he'd cried all the tears out. He pushed his hot face against my chest and it felt like he was trying to burrow his way in. I rubbed his back and told him it was all right, but he wasn't listening, he just needed a good cry and a comfort. When he'd cried himself out I asked if he'd told his mum about all this.

'She's been sad. Steve doesn't come round any more so she's been in her room.'

'You're a right pair at the minute, aren't you?' I said, and he nodded that they were. Emptying himself of the tears seemed to help and he perked up a little. After all that emotion I thought it might do him good to get some fresh air so we played out in the garden and had a few laughs chasing around in the overgrowth for a while, pretending I was a zombie trying to get him, but when it was time for home he fell quiet again.

We walked the normal route back to Jake's house but before we reached Fox Street he veered off track and was heading to the main road.

'Jake?' I said. He stopped and turned round.

'I have to go and get chips,' he said. 'For tea.'

Fair enough. 'You and your mum having fish and chips then?'

'Just me, it's Saturday so she's going out. She doesn't eat when she's going out.'

'Who looks after you when she's out?'

'Nobody, but it's OK, I don't mind. She has to have fun sometimes.'

I couldn't help thinking that people like Jake's mum shouldn't be allowed to have kids. I left him there and started making my way home to spend a silent Saturday night with Mum and our books. But sat down with my book I didn't do much reading. I was thinking about Jake's mum. Trying to work her out. What kind of woman sends a little lad out and tells him not to come back before five? All I'd got from Jake was that she was twenty-six, they lived alone, and she went out at night and left him. I didn't like the thought of her much, but I knew it was wrong to jump to conclusions. It's important to give people a chance. You shouldn't judge without all the evidence. I couldn't concentrate on my reading any more, so I asked Mum if she wanted a game of dominoes but she waved me quiet and carried on with her book. I left her to it and went up to bed early.

The next Saturday I got chance to see Jake's mum for myself. I was at the library and Jake came in and returned some books. He came over to say hello but couldn't hang around; his mum was waiting outside and he was helping her with the shopping. I left it a couple of minutes before I walked out after Jake and followed them further into town. It was obvious where Jake got the skin and bones from – she was made up of nothing else – she could have passed for one of those skinny foreign girl gymnasts. She didn't look much older than some of the sixth-form girls and I wondered for a moment if there was an older sister Jake had forgotten to mention. Her hair fell straight and thin and she was wearing a grey tracksuit which had the word 'Juicy' written across her backside. It didn't look juicy at all. I hung back so there was no chance that Jake would see me and call out, but I didn't need to follow too closely because he'd told me that they always go to the precinct behind the town hall, where they have all the cheap shops.

Even before they made it to the precinct it was easy to see what was going on. Jake was free to run ahead, to cross busy roads without being properly supervised, to walk too close to the road with cars and trucks shooting past. His mum spent most of her time talking into her phone and ignoring him. She snapped at him a few times when he disappeared off in the wrong direction, but he was mainly left alone until it came to bag carrying. As they trudged back in the direction of Fox Street, Jake swung one of the bags a little too high and half of the contents fell out onto the pavement, spilling into the gutter. His mum turned to see what the commotion was. She saw what had happened, shook her head and carried on walking, leaving him there to pick up everything by himself. Jake made sure he had it all and set off after his mum, who was halfway up the road by then. I went back to the library, but I was too angry and couldn't concentrate on anything so I went back home. Later on that night, after I'd thought about it more, I realised I shouldn't be surprised at how she'd treated him – the fact that he walked home alone from school, was always alone in the library, and by himself every Saturday afternoon, gave a clear indication of her idea of parenting. It was clear that she'd had him too young and didn't know what she was doing. It had been ugly to see, but I was glad that I had. At least I knew what I was up against.

12

My favourite-ever vanishing, other than the early one to Neptune, was a vanishing to Iowa. In Iowa I was Roland Harry and I ran a hardware store. The idea came from a film the English teacher, Mrs Lyon Dean, made us watch at the end of one term. I can't remember what it was called, and I didn't get to follow the story too closely because of all the nattering and mucking about, but I could see it was about a massively fat lady and her family who lived in an old wooden house on the outskirts of a small town in America. One of her sons wasn't quite right and he liked to climb up to the top of a water tower, and his older brother always had to go and rescue him, always had to look out for him. Even when he was angry and annoyed with his brother for doing stupid things, you could tell that he still loved him. l liked that, but it wasn't just the story of the film that interested me; it was the landscape: the wide blue skies, the long straight roads, the massive yellow fields and the quiet, dusty towns. It looked like a safe place. The kind of place where you could be born, live and die and never have to come across any trouble if you didn't want to. The kind of place where you sit on your porch at night and watch the sun go down on a quiet day and look forward to more of the same the next day, the day after and for ever.

In the vanishing my hardware store was on the main street in the middle of the town. We sold everything you could think of: mops, buckets, hammers, nails, screws, paint, paintbrushes, locks and hinges, everything. It was a dusty old store with long shady aisles, wooden floors and high shelves. Every space filled with something someone might want. On the off chance we didn't have it in stock we would order it for you – all part of the service. During the week I worked there alone. My wife, Lucy, dropped by with sandwiches at lunch and we would eat them at the counter and chat for a while before she headed back home. At weekends business picked up and I employed a Saturday boy who served, and helped customers with their purchases to their cars, whilst I advised and rummaged through the shelves and the stock room for whatever was needed.

For a while, when the Iowa vanishing was new and fresh, it was a great place to be. I loved settling into bed at night and transporting myself to the middle of America, to my white house with the porch, my store on the main street of a sleepy town, at night my wife next to me, a warm breeze slipping through the room, a dog asleep at the foot of the bed. It was perfect. It was such a good vanishing, so vivid, so calm, that it was one of the few that worked in the daytime too. Sat with my mum eating our tea, neither of us with anything to say, or on a bad day when every thought turned back to the dead little boy, all I needed to do was think of Iowa and I could escape, for a while at least. But vanishings get used up, they wear themselves out through use, and once they're worn out they're empty. You can keep trying to go back, you can keep trying to escape, but it's never the same and eventually they don't work at all. And then you're back to reality with a thump, and you have to wait for inspiration to strike again, you have to wait until you're able to conjure up a whole new vanishing to somewhere else.

13

We started to make something of the house. Well I did. Just the room upstairs where Jake thought Mrs Lorriemore was shot, and where we did the reading and spent most of our time. I'd had my eyes peeled for a while and found it easy to pick stuff up from out and about. The music room at school was being done up and loads was getting chucked so I acted like a magpie and swooped. And then I found a skip outside one of the big houses on Eastham Street. Eastham Street lies about a mile north of the quarry and is the richest street in town. The houses have lawns that need to be mowed with little tractor lawnmowers and the garages are as big as bungalows. All the children from Eastham Street wear the purple uniform of Greenhurst Private School and nobody from my school knows anyone from that school and you never see any of them out and about in town. And you never see anyone from Eastham Street on Eastham Street, just people who don't live there walking their dogs up to the woods, gawping at the big houses on their way. I'd clocked the skip on one of my wanderings. It was sat at the end of a long drive and was filled with stuff that didn't look like it needed to be thrown away at all. I had a rummage, decided what I wanted, and went back when it was dark. But when it came to taking it, when I was stood there, I was nervous. I told myself that nobody would put stuff into a skip that they wanted to keep. The first time though, I still felt like a thief, but nobody shouted and ran from the house, and with the length of the drive I had about a two-minute head start on them anyway. As soon as I left Eastham Street I nipped down a track that leads through Moorland Wood, which eventually gets you to the quarry. It was easy enough to get to the haunted house with little chance of seeing anyone, and if someone did spot an overgrown teenager walking through the night carrying a lamp stand over his shoulder, they probably wouldn't say anything, probably be terrified he would crack them one with it.

The next time Jake was due to visit there were old school chairs, a white plastic garden table, a lamp stand and a little bedside table I thought we could leave stuff in. Of course there was no electricity, but the lamp fitted somehow, and the room looked good.

Jake was made up with it when he saw it, and the first time we spent the afternoon there I had a fair job to drag him away and back to his mother's. But that was something that had been happening before I'd done the room up. For the last few weeks he'd been a bit moody at the start of the afternoon, back to his usual self by mid-afternoon, then back to quiet when it was time to get him home. I thought it might be his mum, he had reason there, or something at school, but he shook his head at both of these things. Then I thought he might be getting bored with our Saturday afternoons, that he'd rather be off somewhere else, but when I broached it with him he shook his head again, and it was a relief to know that it wasn't me causing the upset. It was clear that something wasn't right though, and I wanted to help, but when I tried to get him to speak he would fall quiet and not say a word and the more I pried, the tighter his lips became. I didn't push him too much. Instead I tried to cheer him up and get him back to the happy lad I knew from the first couple of weeks. Each Saturday I would attempt to make the day a bit special. I would spend the week thinking about it, thinking about things that might put a smile on his face, and I would plan the afternoon in my head like a vanishing. And it *was* like a vanishing, only now I had Jake and the

93

house there was a real destination waiting for me, not something I'd just imagined out of thin air. I'd bought doughnuts and sweets, the odd cake. One week I even brought a football along. I thought that if he could practise his skills he might surprise the lads back at school and get to play with Harry again. But it was the blinder leading the blind, and we could barely get the ball from one of us to the other. I could see that he wasn't enjoying it any more than I was, so I threw the ball into the overgrowth and we went back into the house and read one of the horror stories instead. But they didn't appear to be working much lately either. I was stuck and the problem I had was I couldn't ask for advice. *What makes eight-year-old boys moody?* was the question I needed answering. But it wasn't a question I could present to Mum or ask at one of my visits to the library. I knew I would have to work it out for myself. The only thing I could think to do was watch him as closely as possible, keep looking for clues.

14

It might have helped if I'd encountered more of people's problems and struggles, but other than Mum's moods, which I've never found an answer for, I've had little experience. There haven't been friends with problems that have needed sorting out; there haven't really been too many friends at all. I've realised, over the years, that I have a face that lends itself to anonymity. Or perhaps my vanishings have been so successful I have actually started wiping myself out. It has felt that way at times. Mum says I don't draw people; that I'm a dart that bounces back from the board, a magnet that won't pull. She says it's a characteristic inherited from her, which seems unfair to me. Being alone suits her down to the ground but it can drive me mad. Sometimes I want more than books and vanishings and bad memories. Sometimes I want voices and noise and fun to drown everything else out. But it's never happened like that. It has been lonely at times. Of course it has. Fiona has been around since we moved to Raithswaite, and I've been lucky with that, but we can go days without seeing each other, and when we do meet we might just wander around the quarry listening to half a song each through her headphones, not saying a word, and at school we hardly see each other at all. I know she thinks I'm odd, like the rest of them do, but it doesn't seem to bother her as much. I think it's because she doesn't fit either. She's too bright for her dad and her stupid brothers and they hardly speak at all. And whilst loads of people at school want to be her friend because she's so beautiful, she isn't interested in any of them. She plays along, I can see that, but she's waiting for the first opportunity to leg it from Raithswaite. She's biding her time, waiting for the starting pistol, and once she's gone I don't think any of us will ever see her again.

Other friends have been few and far between. I was at St Edmund's Primary School for a year when we moved to Raithswaite and after that I moved to the high school. I can hardly remember a thing about St Edmund's other than it was at the far side of town, but the only primary school in Raithswaite that had any places. The kids and teachers were nice enough to me there, but everyone had known everyone else for years and I was only there for the last few months, and I was quiet and dull so no big friendships blossomed.

Things started off well in my first year at Raithswaite High though, maybe because everyone was new and people were making more of an effort. There were three of us for a while, and we were almost like a gang for a few months. Me, Lewis Johnson and Nathan Pierce. Lewis was a reader, like me, and I'd see him in the library at lunch. We were in the same year and the only two lads from that year in the library all the time and gradually we became friends. A couple of months into the term Nathan turned up in Raithswaite and wandered into the library on his first day and found us. The three of us knocked around together straight away. We even got out and about at lunchtime and started seeing what else the school had to offer. It worked well at first, but gradually I started to feel like a spare part, the weak link. Lewis and Nathan lived on the same estate as each other, and it was on the other side of town to me. They spent weekends and holidays together, staying for tea and sleepovers at each other's houses. They swapped games and music and I hadn't got a clue what they were talking about some of the time. I never felt quite comfortable with the two of them together is the truth. They got on so well, they shared a sense of humour, laughed in all the right places, and I was sometimes slow to catch on, slow to recover from a vanishing. I upset the rhythm. And if it was a bad day, or days, and I was thinking about the little boy, I knew I wasn't much fun to be around, I knew I didn't contribute much. But there were other things too. Their clothes were always brand new and everything they owned was expensive – little names or logos on the left breast, nothing flash, just enough to let you know it cost money, and it was obvious that cash was knocking around in a way that it wasn't in my house. Most of my clothes have always come from the market or the shops in the precinct. And I'm not complaining, cheap clothes never bothered me, but when Mum said you couldn't tell the difference between the clothes I wore and the ones from proper shops I knew that was untrue. Market clothes you can tell a mile off.

I only went round to theirs once. It was all planned. A big Saturday. We were having lunch at Lewis's and tea at Nathan's. Their houses were detached new builds on opposite sides of the same estate. You could hardly tell them apart from the outside and they even smelt the same on the inside. I'd never been surrounded by so many new things before, and I'd never been in houses where everything matched, where everything fitted exactly into the space it sat. It was the same in the lads' bedrooms, everything new and in its place. They told me that they'd got to choose their own furniture and the colour of the walls. I remember being up in Nathan's room and seeing a shelf of books, all the spines facing out into the room, bright and un-broken. I pulled a couple down and opened them up and there wasn't a library marking in sight. In both houses you had to take your trainers off and leave them by the front door. I didn't know that happened and there were holes in my socks where my toenails poked through. Nobody said anything, but I hated being there with my disintegrating socks and my crappy old trainers sat next to their trainers by the front door. Even their mums made me feel out of place. They were bright and friendly, coming back from the shops with bags full of expensive things, handing out treats like it was Christmas. It was the most embarrassing at Nathan's when we had tea. His mum and dad sat with us and we were having spa-ghetti Bolognese. They had a glass of wine each, we all had big glasses of Coke, with ice and lemon, like we were at a restaurant. I'd never had spa-ghetti Bolognese before, it wasn't the kind of thing Mum would cook, and it tasted nice, but I couldn't work out how you were supposed to eat the long spaghetti. They all seemed experts at swizzling it around their forks, but I didn't have the knack. When Nathan's dad saw me struggling he said, 'Tricky isn't it Donald? Do what I do and cut the slippery sods up like this.' He started chopping up his spaghetti, and it was kind of him to pretend like that, but it made me feel more stupid, not even being able to eat like they could. After tea when I stepped onto the thick carpet I wanted to sink and keep sinking down until I was gone. All day I felt like I was an actor on stage, an actor who didn't know what play he was in, never mind know his lines. It was a relief when Nathan's dad eventually drove me home at the end of the day. Me, Nathan and Lewis started seeing less of each other after that. I spent more time back in the library, and they came to visit me there less, and we reached a mutual understanding about the end of the gang without anyone saying anything or anyone getting too upset. Since then there hasn't really been anyone other than Fiona. Looking back over the last four or five years, I don't know what I've been doing with my time other than sitting in a silent house with my silent mum, trying not to think about what happened in Clifton and disappearing to places I've invented in my head. It was good to have Jake.

15

Mum has grown into her silence over the years and only breaks out from it when the hush has built to a point where it has to escape. All the quiet gathers itself together and explodes from her in an inevitable screaming and shouting rage. Anything can set it off – a bill that is bigger than expected, a plate that falls and smashes from the draining board. Something small will be the kindling, but the explosion won't trigger until I provide the spark. I might have ripped the badge from my school blazer, I might have forgotten to wash up a cup, or I could have washed the cup and left the tea towel in the wrong place. She will quickly pounce on the offence and then there is nothing to be done other than stand back and wait until she rages herself out. Anything said during one of these rampages will only prolong the episode, any words offered will be used as fuel and turned against you. The only thing to be done is to stand back and wait. After the eruption she will take herself off to her room and I won't see her until the next day, when she will be back to quiet and sad, and looking at me like I've stolen money from her purse. It wasn't always the case. I remember in Clifton she would sometimes sing along to the radio, she would sometimes have the radio on quite loud. These days the radio only ever mutters quietly – grumpy men discussing news, politics and economics endlessly all day, or she tunes it to a classical station playing gloomy string music and turns the volume down until it sounds like a group of old men, whispering sadly into their beards. I think she's keeping everything quiet so she will hear fresh trouble approaching. So she will know what I've been up to this time before the police knock at the door.

On Thursday nights she writes in her notebook. Thursday nights are the most silent of our silent nights. She boils up a pot of tea, opens a fresh white page and pushes the pen down into the paper. She writes the date in the top left-hand corner of the new page and then relentlessly fills four sheets with closely packed text, hardly pausing for thought. I'm not allowed to see what's written on those pages, and I've no idea where she keeps the journal hidden. I'm dying to know what words she has discovered in herself because I can't imagine what she has to say every week. Mum is unhappy, I know, but it doesn't take an hour to write *I am sad. I hate Raiths-waite. Donald ruined my life.* The only thing that can disrupt the flow of words is noise. The clock ticks too loud for her on writing night. People in the towns over the other side of Denple Hill turn the pages of their books too loudly for her on writing night. Once I got accused of breathing too noisily. Thursday nights I stay in my room and try not to provoke her.

It was a Thursday night when I saw the back of Fiona's head down in the quarry, moving amongst the trees and bushes. It was a relief to have an excuse to get out of the house and I was with her in a few minutes. She unplugged herself from her headphones when she saw me and we fell into step together. We chatted about school and then there was a pause and I was about to ask how her brother was getting on in prison, but she got in a split second quicker.

'I've seen you Donald. You and that little lad. I've seen you a couple of times now, coming and going about the place.'

Guilt tingled my scalp and rushed to the end of each fingertip and I didn't know why. I nodded, like I was agreeing with a point she was making, but I didn't know what to say.

'So who is he Donald?' she asked.

On the second 'd' of 'Donald' a handbrake was released and from nowhere a lie started coming out of my mouth that was so convincing I believed it as I was creating it. Jake Dodd was a lad I had got to know through Raithswaite Library reading clubs. There were two groups. Ours, the teenage group, had each been given a kid to mentor from the younger group. We were supposed to encourage them to read books they wouldn't normally read, to stretch themselves. I'd been assigned to Jake and got friendly with him and his mum and she asked me to watch him sometimes when she had to be off doing other stuff. It was so convincing and boring an explanation that I knew Fiona was believing it as I was telling her. I finished and she told me I deserved a medal. We carried on walking through the quarry and she described visiting her brother at the prison.

'It stank Donald. All those teenage boys in their orange sweaters with nobody to keep clean for. I tried not to touch anything but I still had to have a shower when I got home.'

'I bet they liked the look of you,' I said. My body and brain was still fizzing from the question about Jake, and I said it without thinking, but Fiona stopped walking suddenly and said, 'Some of them didn't even pretend Donald. They just stared. And when I stared back they didn't even blink. One lad spotted me as I came in, and he watched me walk all the way across the room and sit down opposite my brother. He never took his eyes off me. I don't like being stared at at the best of times but that was horrible. The thing is you don't know what they're in there for. You don't know what they've done.'

She shuddered as we walked on and put her arm through mine. It was the first time we'd ever really touched and it felt very grown-up. I knew it didn't mean anything, but it felt good. Later on that night, as I lay in bed, I thought that maybe I wouldn't go and see Jake on Saturday as usual. I would try and stay away from the school too. Let the little ones play by themselves for a while, they would be OK. And Jake would be fine without me checking up on him. I would plan a vanishing instead. I would go to the library and get the *Times Atlas* out and start to look for suitable destinations.

But come Saturday lunchtime there I was, sat on the bench at the playground waiting for him. I couldn't let him down like that. The thought of him turning up and being left by himself with the afternoon to get through made me too sad. And it was a good job I was there. He walked into the playground, looked up to find me, and I saw it straight away – a shiny lump above his right eye, as big as an Adam's apple, as purple as a plum. We didn't walk up to the house like we normally did; he looked too tired for walking, so we stayed on the bench at the playground. He said that Harry had done it. Smacked him one in a fight, so Jake had smacked him one back, and then they went for each other and had both ended up in trouble. 'What were you fighting about anyway?' I asked him. Jake said he didn't know. They were just fighting. He yawned heavily and there were dark patches under his eyes that weren't bruises.

'You tired Jake?'

'Yeah, I don't sleep so well when Mum goes out.'

'You don't like being alone?'

'I don't mind in the day, but not at night much, when she doesn't come back.'

'She doesn't come back all night?'

'Sometimes she doesn't. It's OK. We spoke about it. She's always got her phone.'

She's always got her phone. I didn't know what to say.

'How long has she been staying out all night Jake?'

'Steve doesn't come around any more. It started after that. At first she stayed in her room all the time but then she started going out. Mainly Fridays and Saturdays. Sometimes Thursdays too.'

I was angry but I knew to keep quiet. When I was calm enough to speak normally I asked Jake if she would be out that night.

'She always goes to the Social on a Saturday,' Jake said.

'The Social on Wellgate?' He nodded that was the place. We didn't stay out too long that afternoon. I sent Jake home early and told him to get some rest. He should try and sleep if he wasn't going to be sleeping later.

16

The Social on Wellgate is slipped between a shoe shop and a florist. It has a narrow, brown-tiled front and a dark corridor that leads to the unknown. Pubs are frowned on in our house and I can't remember an occasion when Mum or I have ever been in one. A few pubs around town have shut up recently, they have grey grilles over the windows, but the ones in the centre are still open and ready for action. I settled myself out of the way, high up on the stone steps of Parrot's Dentists where I could see up to the Red Lion and the Wagon, across to the Social, and down to the Dog, the Castle, and Romero's fast food place. I'd brought a book with me because I knew it was going to be a long night, but I'd only been there twenty minutes or so before the drinkers began to appear, the street started getting busy and I had to put the book away. There was evidently a one-way system in place for drinking in Raithswaite and everyone travelled in a downward direction. The general order was

Red Lion, Wagon, Social, Dog and then the Castle. I watched people moving in packs from pub to pub, chatting and pushing each other along. There were the smokers to watch too, coming in and out, borrowing lights, falling into conversation, groups merging together and slowly dissolving before growing again. I had to watch closely to make sure I didn't miss Jake's mum, but I was enjoying myself, it was fun to watch all this toing and froing in my town centre on a Saturday night. I gulped it down. *This* is what people did at the weekend, I understood. They didn't all sit in with their library books and classical radio turned so low it sounded like an orchestra playing in a cave over the other side of a hill. They didn't glower at the closed curtains when people shouted to each other in loud voices in the street. They *were* the loud voices in the street. It looked good fun to my eyes. Some of the women were spectacular in their shiny dresses and heels with their hair, big, smooth and glossy, almost sparkling. You could see the confidence a mile off as they strode their way along, bright shoes pointing forward. I enjoyed myself sitting up there, watching the night happen around me.

I'd been on the steps about an hour before I saw Jake's mum making her way down the road. She was alone and unlike most people she bypassed the first two pubs and headed straight to the Social. She had on a dress and a pair of heels and there was colour on her cheeks, a redness to her lips, but there was none of the glamour or glitz of the other women to her. She was wearing the uniform, but it didn't work like it should. Her skinniness let her down. Her flesh seemed limited to the amount that would just about cover her bones, and it made her look pinched and mean. There was nothing luxurious about her at all, not like the other women, who laughed and linked arms with each other and looked at men and didn't care when they were spotted looking. Those women seemed to be having the time of their lives, like it was a Hollywood night out, not Raithswaite on a Saturday. Jake's mum walked with her handbag clutched to her front, her eyes down to the pavement, glancing up only when she needed to, taking tight little steps through the town. And whilst I'm one to sympathise with the underdogs of the world, with the people in their cheap clothes, I couldn't do it this time. All I could think of was Jake, at home, chips in his tummy, probably already in bed, lying under the sheets thinking about ghosts and ghouls and the terrors of the night.

I kept my watch on the Social front door and

people came and went but Jake's mum wasn't one of them. At half eleven people started oozing out of the narrow entrance in a steady stream, looking for taxis, heading off down the road or joining the growing crowd at Romero's. Town was shutting up and I had no idea where she'd got to. It wasn't until the street was much quieter and Romero's was down to its last few customers, and I was thinking that I must have missed her surely, that I saw her again. She came out of the Social with a huge man, a pony-tailed man in a black shirt. He turned, pulled down a shutter over the entrance and locked a padlock. They walked back up Wellgate together, up towards the library and the square, and I followed. She nestled herself in towards him, he dropped one of his bulky arms around her tiny shoulder and I thought it must feel as heavy as wet rope. They walked slowly, in no rush to get anywhere, her looking up at him like he was the Blackpool illuminations, eyes wide, her lips smiling. I trailed them all the way to the wrong side of town and a house on the Faraday Estate. I thought about Jake, alone in the dark little house on Fox Street. I waited across the road for twenty minutes and when other people started turning up with cans and bottles, and music started seeping out from the house, I knew that nobody would be leaving any time soon.

I didn't want to scare him but I could think of no way of getting to him that would scare him less. I picked the smaller stones, but he still looked terrified when he pulled back the curtain and peered down into the backyard. I dropped the rest of the stones to the ground and waved for him to come down. A minute later he opened the back door wide enough for me to squeeze through. There was a warm fuzziness to him and he looked slow on his feet and I knew I'd woken him up. I followed him through to the front room and we sat down. He reached for the light switch but I told him he'd better leave it. He looked at me blankly and I realised he might have thought he was dreaming. 'I was walking through town,' I told him, 'and I saw your mum coming the opposite way, and I didn't like the thought of you all alone so I thought I'd better pop in and check you were all right.'

'You saw my mum?'

'Yeah, she was out in town. I don't think she'll be coming back for a while.'

'Is it still night time?' he asked, and I was annoyed at myself for being as inconsiderate as his mum.

'It's after twelve,' I told him, 'it's the middle of the

night and I didn't like the thought of you all alone in here. I thought you'd be frightened.'

'I don't like being by myself,' he said.

'Listen Jake, it's important you don't tell your mum I was here. I think she was upset at leaving you alone, and we don't want to make it worse by letting her know I had to come and check up on you. We don't want to upset her more, do we?'

He nodded and I couldn't think of anything else to say and we sat on the couch in silence for a while, and it was like a bad date in a film and I regretted coming.

Eventually he asked, 'Are we going to the haunted house?'

I'd been stupid. I shouldn't have come like this. I should have told him what I'd been planning. The idea was to make him feel better, not unsettle him more. I told him it was far too late for the haunted house.

'We should get you back to bed,' I told him.

I pulled him up and we walked down the hall to the stairs. I had a good look around as he shuffled slowly along, and the house looked clean enough, as much as I could tell in the gloominess anyway, I had to give her credit for that. But there were no pictures or plants anywhere that I could see; there was nothing to make the place homely at all. It was brighter upstairs with the landing light and Jake's bedroom light already on. His room was in more of a state than the rest of the house, but that was just young lads, I understood you couldn't blame her for that. He climbed into bed and I sat down on the edge of his mattress and looked around the room. There wasn't much to suggest it was a little boy's room. If it wasn't for the clothes scattered around you would've had a job to know at all; there were no toys or books anywhere. I didn't notice the drawings until he'd snuggled himself up in bed. They were stuck above the bed and my heart slipped into my throat when I saw what he'd drawn in one of them. Pride of place in the middle of all of them was a drawing of me and Jake in the upstairs room of the haunted house. A big white ghost flying above us. I pointed and asked, 'Is that one of us?' Jake turned and looked and nodded and said, 'In the haunted house.' It was a mixture of feelings. I was pleased it was on his wall, that he'd thought about it enough to turn it into a picture, but it made me uneasy to see it in full view. 'It's brilliant that, Jake,' I told him. 'You've got a real talent there.' He curled up in bed and hugged himself and said, 'Thanks.'

'Would you mind if I borrowed it for a few days so I can do a copy?'

'You can have it. Are you staying?'

'Shall I stay until you're asleep?'

He nodded and put his thumb in his mouth and was quiet and still in seconds. I didn't know he was a thumb sucker. I waited with him until I was sure he was asleep, tucked him in a little better and took the drawing down off the wall. I rearranged the other pictures so there was no obvious gap, had one more look at Jake and left the room. I kept the landing light on and walked down the stairs to the dark ground floor, through the kitchen and let myself out of the back door. I was tired by then, but not too tired to check. I made my way home via the house on the Faraday Estate. There was still music playing and loud voices coming from inside. A man and a woman left by the front door and snuck around the back holding hands and giggling. I left them to it and dragged myself home. I didn't get in until about two in the morning and I knew I'd be for it when Mum got hold of me, but I also knew that it didn't really matter much.

Trouble is worth facing down for something you believe in.

17

I should have been braver in the face of trouble once before. The whole thing still upsets me to this day and afterwards I decided I would always try to do the right thing, regardless of how much bother it could lead to. I've always loved animals but we were never allowed a pet. Mum said animals were mucky.

'Cats aren't,' I told her, 'cats are clean.'

'Just because an animal has the instinct to bury its own mess doesn't mean it's clean Donald,' she said. 'Think about where they walk, what they get into, and then think of them prancing around the house on their filthy paws. And when you're not there, jumping on your kitchen surfaces, sleeping on your pillows. Cats are sneaky creatures.'

The closest I had to a pet was Mr Mole's dog, Scruffy, who I used to walk sometimes, but even Scruffy wasn't allowed in our house, so I knew a pet of my own was unlikely. But the day I found the kitten I thought for a silly few seconds that if I took

him home and Mum saw him, she might be per-
suaded to let me keep him. She would, of course,
have screamed at the sight and made me get it out
of the house straight away, but this was before the
trouble and before all hope was extinguished from
our world. *Maybe*, I thought, she would see the kitten
and her heart would melt. But I never managed to
get the kitten to the house. I wasn't alone when I
found him; I was with Reece Aighton.

It was a hot day and I'd been riding my bike on the
waste ground behind the backs of the houses, wondering what to do for the rest of the afternoon, when
Reece turned up. He lived in the new houses they'd
built at the top of Hawthorne Road and was in the
year above me at school. He never spoke to me at
school but we occasionally bumped into each other
at weekends, or in the holidays, and mucked around
together for a bit before he would turn nasty and I
would sneak off.

He was rich. His dad drove a little silver sports car
and in the summer they would zoom up the road
with the top down, both of them wearing sunglasses,
looking straight ahead, like they owned every house
on the hill. Reece always had money in his pocket
and that afternoon an ice-cream van had been round
and he'd bought himself a ninety-nine and a can. We

put our bikes down and were sat by the corner of one of the garages so he could eat his ice cream and drink his drink. We were throwing stones to see if we could hit a bin that was sitting at the side of one of the garages opposite. Reece was annoyed because I'd hit it twice and he hadn't got close. He didn't like to lose, especially not to someone like me. He finished eating and stood up as a sign that he was going to start taking the game seriously. But then I hit the bin for a third time and his patience snapped and he started throwing stones at me. They stung and I told him to stop, but he was treating it like it was part of the game and said that I was being a crybaby. I was about to pick up my bike and ride off when we heard a small crying sound coming from behind one of the garages. Reece put his stones in his pocket and we went to explore. By the time we got behind the garage the noise had stopped and we had a root round but couldn't find anything. Just as we were about to give up and head off the crying started again, near to my feet, and I got down on my hands and knees and had a look through the long grass. I found a grey kitten about a foot away from the garage wall, sat like a tiny statue, his tail wrapped neatly around his feet. Reece was at my side quickly and leant forward to give the kitten a stroke but a sharp claw shot up and swiped at his hand before he made contact. Reece pulled his hand away and held it up to have a look. There was a small tear with little blots of blood bubbling through.

'He's vicious,' he said.

'Probably just scared,' I said. 'He must have lost his mum.'

Reece peered down at him and said, 'He doesn't have a collar. Do you think he's a wild cat?'

There were sometimes feral cats that ventured from the fields into the back lane and ate food from the bins.

'He must be,' I said.

Reece leant forward to try and stroke him again but this time the kitten got his claw in deep and Reece cried out in pain and took a swing with his foot. The kitten flew back and hit the wall of the garage and stayed put where he landed, looking stunned.

'Don't kick him!' I said.

'He needed to learn a lesson,' Reece said, and shoved me over. I got myself up and looked at his face and saw that he was blinking away a tear. He looked as shocked as the kitten. He inspected his hand which had turned pinky-red around the edge of the new tear. He kicked the wall of the garage and shouted something that wasn't a word and I knew that things were going to get worse and it was time to leave. I started to walk away. I was hoping to get rid of Reece and then come back and check on the kitten, maybe even rescue him and take him home.

'Let's go. You should get home and get your hand cleaned up,' I said. Reece held up his hand like he was showing me a stab wound.

'I can't let him get away with that,' he said, 'don't be stupid Donald.'

He threw a stone at me and then hit me on the arm. 'He could attack anyone. Just think if he went for my little brother.' I'd seen Reece's little brother. A curly-haired four-year-old with a big head and thick arms and legs who would terrify the kitten more than the other way round. 'He'll be one of those gypsy cats anyway,' he said, 'and they carry diseases. I'll probably have to have an injection for my hand. I might get admitted to hospital.' He kicked the wall of the garage again. 'We should put a stop to him before he attacks anyone else.' He took a stone out of his pocket and threw it at the kitten. The kitten was trying to walk off, but was still dazed from the kick and was limping. 'Go and get some stones,' Reece told me. 'You can't leave me to do all the work. We need to stop him.'

'He's hurt. We should leave him. We'll get into trouble.' I could hear the whine in my voice and I knew that Reece would hear it too. He turned on me. 'He's hurt? I'm hurt! Is a dirty little gypsy cat more important to you than me?' He hit me on my arm harder than before and rubbed a stone into my head until I cried out.

'Go and get some stones,' he said, his face close to mine, his breath sweet and cold.

'I don't think we should,' I said.

'Go and get some stones,' he said, again. When I didn't make a move Reece pushed me to the ground and we wrestled for a bit, but he was much stronger than I was. He pinned me down, his knees on my arms, his hands pushing my hands to the ground. He leant forward, brought up a glob of phlegm from the back of his throat, and spat it in my face. 'Go and get some stones.' I walked to the front of the garages, wiping my face clean with my sleeve as much as I could. My bike was lying on the ground. I looked up and saw the roof of my house and my bedroom window. I was ready to make a run for it when Reece appeared behind me. He pushed my arm up against my back until I thought it would snap and said, 'Don't make me tell everyone you were a pissy-pants coward Donald.' He let go and I picked a handful of stones up from the gravel and followed him behind the garage. I was praying that the kitten had run off, but he hadn't. Even then, when Reece threw the first stone as hard as he could, I was still thinking that I might be able to stop it.

A few months later, after the little boy, when I was back at school, I heard a rumour about myself. Reece had told everyone what happened, but he changed the story, so that it was me who was intent on killing the kitten and him who had tried to stop it. He told them that I smashed the kitten's head open with a big rock and then kicked it into a stream. I don't think anyone would have believed him even a few days before, but when I came back to the school I was already a killer and the kids were happy to start believing anything about me. Within a couple of days I'd gone from being a normal little kid who didn't know how to stand up to a bad lad, to a murderer and a kitten killer. A psycho killer.

18

It was the early hours by the time I got back from the Faraday Estate and Sunday started with Mum shouting me awake, accusing me of drink and drugs and anything else she could think of through the fog of her fury. I tried not to respond but she was in no mood to have a one-sided fight and I rose to the occasion and we shouted until we ran out of voice and argument. We were both left empty, exhausted and trembling. She didn't have the energy to slam my door properly when it was over. I spent the rest of the day in my room, lying on the bed, ignoring books and homework, worrying about Jake.

Monday I went to find him on his walk home from school. I caught him on Pickup Street, by the entrance to the park. 'Did she come back?' He pulled up short, surprised. I'd jumped in too fast, no explanation. I needed to calm down. Sometimes I've got so lost in what's going on in my head that I forget that not everyone is thinking the same thing. I fell into step with him and we had a chat about his day at school instead. He was in a good mood. The football lads had decided that Harry wasn't one of them after all and had sent him back to Jake with his new ginger spikes flattened down and his shiny trainers all scuffed up, so it was back to the two of them hanging around by the tree, chatting and messing around. And best of all, Harry hadn't told Jake that his breath stank or that his clothes were rubbish since his return. I was pleased for Jake, I was, but I couldn't help thinking what a little bastard Harry was to treat someone the way he'd treated Jake – turning his back on Jake for the football lads one minute and then crawling back the next, when they'd had enough of him. But I didn't say anything, it was just good to see Jake a little happier, more like his old self. When Jake had finished telling me about Harry, I tried again.

'So did your mum come back in the end then on Sunday?' I asked him.

'She came back. She took me out for tea,' he said.

'What time did she get back?'

'About lunchtime and then she went to bed. When she got up she said she was starving and we went out for tea. I had a burger.'

I didn't say anything for a while and then Jake said, 'It's OK. I don't mind.'

I knew he was lying then. I could see the little man

in him pushing to get out, trying to show himself as brave. I was proud of him but I wasn't fooled.

'It's not right Jake. You shouldn't be left alone, you know. You're still a little lad.'

He was quiet for a while. 'I don't like being alone. I don't mind in the day, but at night when it's dark, I hear noises. I don't like that. I leave the light on in my room but I still know that it's dark everywhere else and then I get scared about what's out in the dark.'

'Well, at night it's easy to be scared by things that wouldn't be scary in the daytime,' I told him. 'If you hear a bump during the day you don't even think about it, but at night it becomes something else, doesn't it?' I said. I tried to make him laugh. 'It becomes the monster on the other side of the door.' I made a face and did an impression of a monster lumbering along, but I didn't get a smile.

'At night I think about that man who shot the woman through the floorboards in the haunted house, and I think that he's downstairs in my house. I think that he's going to come and shoot me. When my mum isn't there I sometimes turn all the lights on in every room, but I'm still scared. If I'm upstairs I think he's downstairs and if I'm downstairs I hear noises upstairs, and then I think he's up there waiting for me.'

I'd been stupid. That was my fault.

I put my arm around his shoulder and said, 'You're a brave lad you know.'

We were getting close to his street and it was time I left. I asked him if he wanted to meet in the library or at the playground on Saturday, and we agreed on the playground. We set a time and I headed off home, thinking what to do about Jake as I went.

When I got back Mum was still in a black mood and her festering infected the house and filled the rooms with anger and frustration. She was fed up when I was in the house too much; she was fed up when I wasn't there enough. I usually found it a tricky balance to maintain, but lately I hadn't bothered to try and make it balance at all. She was in the type of mood where you could do no right. Even if you just sat there and said nothing you would do it in a way that would rile her. When she's like that there's nothing to be done. A bird singing in a tree in the backyard will get the door slammed on it. A neighbour whistling in their bedroom two doors down will be cursed. In the past I've tolerated these moods, tiptoed around them, tried to help ease them on their way, but I didn't have the patience any more. I was fed up with her acting as if she was the only person in the world who ever felt sad and lonely and frustrated and desperate. And with all the thinking I needed to do I was in no mood for her. She started as soon as I walked in through the front door, so I was out of the back door five seconds later. Her voice was silenced by the slammed door, but it was only silenced for a second before the door swung open and bellowed threats of retribution hit the back of my head. I walked as fast as I could away from the house without turning round. I didn't care what she had to say; she could save it for Thursday night and put it all in her fucking notebook. I had to get out, I had to think and I couldn't think whilst she was stewing away in the corner of the back room. All of a sudden I knew what I needed. It hit me like a snowball in the face. I needed to see Fiona.

The quarry was deserted. No sign of her. Just when I needed to see her the most. That saying: *a watched pot never boils* is rubbish because a watched pot boils in the same time as an ignored pot, but they should write a saying about never bumping into someone when you want to, because that's something that's true. I decided to go and knock on her door. It was something I hadn't done for years, but I really wanted to see her. I walked down into the quarry and up and out of the far side, across the

field, over the fence, and was on the top of Salthill
Road in five minutes. There were about sixty houses
stretching out in front of me in a line. All ex-council,
all exactly the same, and I couldn't remember what
number she lived at. I wandered down the street and
struck lucky – the union jack was still hanging in the
front garden, battered and worn, like it had seen service. Fiona's dad had put it up years ago when an
Asian family moved into the house next door, and
it had stayed there since, even after the Asian family had long moved on. It was in a sorry state now –
the white had stained to grey and the red had faded
to a light pink and smudged its way out of the shape
of a cross. I had second thoughts stood outside the
house. Their place never looked welcoming and I
wasn't keen on her dad or her brothers, but I did
want to see Fiona. I knocked and immediately started saying to myself: *Please let it be Fiona, please let it
be Fiona, please let it be Fiona*, but it was her younger brother, Tyler, who opened the door. He looked
me up and down and took a bite from a piece of
bread. 'Yeah?' he said and chewed. It had been years
since he'd last seen me and he didn't have a clue
who I was. I asked if Fiona was in and he smiled an
open-mouthed smile, the bread looking like mashed
potato in his mouth. 'You dirty bastard,' he said. He

bellowed for Fiona before disappearing back into the front room, the door slamming behind him. I heard Fiona swear from somewhere in the house and a few seconds later she was stomping down the stairs. She reached the bottom and told me to stay where I was and vanished behind a door. She appeared a moment later with her big jacket on, pulled the door closed behind her and we set off walking. I got a good look at her as she'd come down the stairs and it was one of the few days when she wasn't wearing any make-up, and I thought she looked tired. But out in the daylight, with the sun shining on us, she looked more beautiful than I'd ever seen her. I had a lump in my throat at the sight of her. She was wearing a pair of jeans, a red and blue checked shirt and her big jacket. She looked so perfect that I wanted to build a brick wall around her so nothing bad could ever touch her. We walked through the late afternoon sun and although it was still warm, she huddled into her jacket and wrapped her arms around herself. I had the thought then that no matter what happened in my life, I would always remember this moment, walking away from Fiona's house with her looking as beautiful as she did, and the sun on our backs and the town still and quiet, like God had pressed the pause button and we were the only people it hadn't paused. I asked her if she was OK and she said she was, 'but you get rid of one dickhead brother and the younger one steps into his shoes immediately.' I told her I was sorry but she shrugged my apology away. 'How come you aren't a massive prick anyway Donald? You're a bloke, you're the right age. Why aren't you trying to grab my arse and getting drunk and fighting and being a dick?' I told her the truth: 'My mum would explode.' She laughed and linked her arm through mine.

We walked down Waddington Road, heading away from town and towards the river. After the road bends left it bends right and you end up looking down onto the Hoddale as it runs its way past the fringes of the town and further out of the valley. To see it below, nestling between the fields, you wouldn't believe it was running water. It looked like a country road winding along down there, and even as we got closer it was running so slowly it hardly looked like it was moving at all. After we'd climbed over the stile at the bottom of the hill and walked a few feet alongside the river Fiona said, 'Come on Donald. What's up? What's bothering you?'

Just then a car shot over the narrow bridge behind us, its engine straining hard, the tyres squealing as it rounded the corner. The noise made us jump and we turned to see the car speed off, its back end swinging from side to side. A woman was stood on the bridge with her daughter, the car must have gone right past them. The little girl was howling and pushing her face into her mum's skirt. You could see the woman was shaken too, but she was trying to encourage the girl off the bridge, to where the road widened and the pavement started. The girl wouldn't let go of the skirt and the woman had to tear her hands away, so she could pick her up and carry her off the bridge. When I could see they were safely on the pavement I moved to the edge of the river, picked up some stones and started throwing them as hard as I could into the water.

'Are you OK Donald?' Fiona had followed me and was stood behind me. I nodded but carried on throwing stones.

'You seem a little wired,' she said.

I did feel wired. That was the right word for it. I felt taut. Tight. Too much energy and nothing to do with it. I felt like I could run right back to Clifton. I felt like I couldn't breathe and couldn't run a step. I felt like every moment was the moment three seconds before you're sick when you're confused and in pain and want to escape your body. I wanted to tell her about the little boy in Clifton. I want to tell her that I killed a little boy and that I wasn't even that bothered for a while afterwards because I didn't mean to do it, and I was told he would be in heaven and that seemed all right to me at the time. I wanted her to know that I wasn't a bad person because I didn't shake and cry and wail when I'd found out he'd died. I just didn't know what I'd done. I hadn't a clue what I'd done. And then we disappeared and Mum would never let it be mentioned so it was never mentioned. But now the silence made me want to scream until my throat tore. I wanted her to know that it would feel good to walk through the middle of town screaming: I KILLED A LITTLE BOY, I KILLED A LITTLE BOY, over and over until everyone knew and there was nobody left to tell. And I wanted to tell her about Jake. I wanted to talk about Jake. A great little lad and nobody cared. Nobody saw what was going on. But what I really wanted her to understand was how it feels to live like you're living in a diving bell, where you're trapped and can't move and things are only going to get tighter and smaller for as long as you're alive until you're the smallest Russian doll in a set of a hundred Russian dolls buried deep in a box in the back garden of a house where nobody has ever lived. I wanted to tell her that I didn't feel well and hadn't done for a long time. I stopped walking. I told her I wanted to go home. She looked at me but didn't say anything and we turned and started walking back towards the bridge and Waddington Road. When we reached her house Fiona took my hands and said, 'Donald, if you need someone to talk to, come and see me. I know things aren't always easy for you, but whenever you need to, come and talk to me.' She put her arms around me and hugged me and I hugged her back and the feel and the smell of her was the best thing that had happened to me for years. I blinked back tears and a moment later she was behind a closed door.

I didn't go home. I went back into town and walked to Gillygate Primary. I walked up to the railings and looked onto the yard. Without any of the children tearing around it looked like a place I'd never seen before. I tried to picture them: Jake and Harry over by the tree, the football lads over the other side and the little girls skipping around it all. But it was impossible to imagine so much life in such a silent space and the emptiness of it made me feel worse so I left. I walked to Jake's street and had a peer at his house, but I couldn't see any sign of life there either. I did a circuit of the town and ended up back at the quarry and now my body was tired but my brain still wasn't slowing. I lay down under a tree and watched the empty quarry and thought about Jake. And then I started thinking about the little boy back in Clifton.

He was two and a half years old. He lived with his mum and dad at the bottom of Hawthorne Road, number five. We lived at the top, number seventy-five. His mum and dad have split up since it happened – that's common after losing a child, very few relationships survive something like that. But divorce is common anyway these days so who knows what would have happened without the tragedy. They loved him very much – I did know that. I used to see them in the park in Clifton, pushing him on the swings, or they would be sliding him down the small slide, one of them letting him go from the top, the other catching him at the bottom, making him squeal with excitement. We'd never spoken before it happened and we didn't speak afterwards. I thought they might come and see me, to get my side of the story, but they must have got a version of that from the police. And then, of course, there was the trouble in their garden at midnight. They weren't going to come after that.

I often think of them. Wonder how they're doing. I know they must blame themselves for what happened. They *must* blame themselves. I hope they do. They have to at least share some of the blame with me. Every time I think about it I always come back to the same point. They shouldn't have let him get outside. They should have been more vigilant. More careful. Maybe that's why they split up. Maybe one of them thought the other one was more to blame and that ruined the relationship. Maybe the one who was more to blame has trouble breathing sometimes too. Perhaps they've never had any real friends since it happened either and aren't allowed to tell people about it for fear of being judged. It would serve them right. I'm being cruel, I know, but sometimes I want to be. Slowly, gradually, over the years, it's ruined me. And it's been clever that way. It let me think for a while that the consequences were manageable. That reason and clear thinking could keep it at bay. But you can't keep your mind as strong as fortress walls for ever. You will wake up in the middle of the night and the walls to your brain will be as mushy as gravied potato. Some nights you will dream, and you can't stop dreams. Some mornings when you wake you'll be attacked before you get a chance to raise your guard. And after each attack it takes longer to rebuild the walls, and you know that there will be another attack on its way and you get tired and it becomes harder to keep your head above water, and you start to wonder if trying to keep your head above water is worth it any more. Fiona was worth it. Jake was worth it. I knew that. What Jake's mum didn't seem to understand was that every step he took could be his last. She appeared oblivious to the fact that little boys can go from alive to dead in a second. That risk is everywhere. I'd learnt early that death isn't only something that you slip into in old age, it isn't something that sits below the surface of the world and tiptoes in at the end of a long life. Death is now. Death is present. It's with babies and kittens as much as it's with the old and ruined. It's there on the sunniest day of the year and it isn't ever going to go away for any of us. The little boy I killed was called Oliver Thomas.

Eventually the quarry turned blue, the trees turned black, the birds stopped singing and I grew cold. It was time to go home. I went in through the back door and straight up to my bedroom. I made enough noise so she would know I was back, but she didn't even come and shout. I couldn't sleep. I was wired to the moon, as fizzy as a dropped can. I found it hard to catch my breath, to get air properly into my lungs. Thoughts wouldn't settle and ran into and over each other and I didn't even attempt to find any sleep. Everything, all of it, such a mess. I didn't know where to start.

19

The problems with my breathing began when I was ten years old. We hadn't been in Raithswaite long the first time it happened and there was no forewarning, nothing to suggest what was coming, so when I woke in the middle of the night feeling like I was suffocating, unable to get air into my lungs, it was terrifying. I tried to think my way through the panic. I couldn't breathe, you need air to be able to breathe, and all the air is outside. I opened my bedroom window and pushed my head out into the cold night, but it made no difference; even though oxygen was all around me I couldn't get any of it through my nose and into my chest. I was drowning inside myself. My panic trebled at this realisation. I banged through to Mum's room, slammed the light on and shouted, 'I can't breathe, I can't breathe!' Before she had chance to do anything I charged down the stairs, flung open the front door and ran out into the street. I fell to my hands and knees, gasping, still trying to get air into my lungs.

Mum followed me out, grabbed my shoulders and pulled me up. She held my head in her hands and looked me in the eye and told me to stop panicking. I didn't know what she was talking about, I wasn't panicking; I was dying. 'I can't breathe,' I gasped, 'I'm going to die.' She told me she'd rung an ambulance and that we should wait inside where it was warm. She helped me into the house. The operator on the phone had told Mum that I should have a glass of warm milk before the ambulance arrived. 'A glass of warm milk?' I was unsure. How could I drink when I couldn't breathe? Mum made me sit with my head between my knees while she warmed the milk in a pan. We'd been sat at the kitchen table for thirty minutes before I realised that no ambulance had been called, no rescue was coming. But at some point in that half an hour I'd remembered how to breathe again. I was still shaky and scared, but my lungs were working and my nose was allowing air to pass into them. When I finished the milk Mum took me upstairs and put me to bed and told me I needed to calm down. 'If you let yourself get wound up like this you'll be in for a very long life.' I lay in bed frozen stiff, expecting death to return at any moment. But I did make it through the night and by lunchtime the next day I'd started to forget about it, forget how terrified I'd felt.

Two weeks later it happened again, and then again a couple of days after that. It started to happen so regularly that it was a relief to get through a day without feeling I was suffocating. Each time I was sure that I really was dying, that all the other times had been leading up to this one, and that now survival was impossible. But Mum didn't believe me. She told me it was a reaction to what had happened back in Clifton. She said my mind was playing tricks on me and I just needed to calm myself down. 'Stress can do funny things to your body,' she said. I'd never heard anything so stupid. I didn't *think* I couldn't breathe; I *couldn't* breathe. I couldn't get air into my lungs. It was nothing to do with stress; something had gone wrong with my body and unless it was sorted out I would die. After much pestering and pleading I was finally allowed to see a doctor, but she made me promise that I wouldn't mention Clifton. 'If you breathe a word about that they'll want to get inside your head. They'll want you to tell them all about it and how it feels and that will set you back.' I didn't want to mention Clifton, I had no interest whatsoever in mentioning Clifton. I wanted help breathing and staying alive. Clifton was the last thing on my mind right then.

The doctor was an old man with a white beard. He looked like Father Christmas.

'What's brought you here today then Donald?' he asked.

'He says that he can't breathe and he's dying,' my mum said.

'Is that true Donald? You think you're dying?'

I nodded.

'That sounds serious. Let's have a look at you.'

He asked me to take my shirt off and pushed a stethoscope to my chest, then my back, and listened. 'Take a deep breath now Donald please.' Then he held my tongue down with a little wooden spatula and shone a torch in my throat and my ears. He told me to breathe into a plastic tube as hard as I could and made a note of the result. He took my pulse and blood pressure and asked me to do twenty star jumps and ten press-ups.

'How's your breathing now?' he asked.

'Fine,' I said. 'But sometimes it isn't. Sometimes I can't breathe.'

He made some notes on his computer and looked at me and said, 'There's nothing wrong with you Donald. You're as healthy as any ten-year-old child I've seen.'

Despair hit me. Tears started to come. If a doctor

didn't believe me, how was I going to get help from anyone? He saw my distress and cocked his head at me. 'I'm just going to ask your mum a few questions Donald. Is that OK?'

I nodded.

'Is he an anxious child?'

'He has his moments,' my mum said.

'Has there been anything recently that could have caused him upset?'

'We have just moved here from another town. He's started a new school.'

'Is that it Donald? Do you miss your old friends?'

He was so far away from understanding that it felt impossible to steer him in the right direction. I didn't say a word.

'It's a big change for a young lad. Especially if he is a bit sensitive. It will take time for him to adjust. Give it a few months and he'll be charging around Raithswaite like he was born and bred here. Physically there's nothing wrong with him. Nothing at all. Get him playing football, get him playing outside, wear him out. He'll be so tired that he'll forget he's supposed to be dying.'

He smiled at us both and Mum stood up to leave.

It happened again that afternoon at school. Dread filled me from the inside. 'I can't breathe,' I told Mrs

Sutton. She sat me down in the school office and made me breathe into a brown paper bag. She rang my mum but my mum refused to come and pick me up. She told Mrs Sutton that we'd been to the doctor and there was nothing wrong with me. I was putting it on for attention, she said, and they should send me back to class. Mrs Sutton didn't send me back to class straight away. She left me with a glass of water and my brown paper bag and I sat on a chair outside the office for the rest of the lesson. I carried that brown paper bag around everywhere after that day. I never left the house without it. I was convinced that it was the only thing that could save my life.

It took me years to work out that I was suffering from panic attacks. I heard a woman interviewed on the radio and her words froze me to the spot. She was describing exactly what had been happening to me for years, and those two simple words summed up the terror so well. Panic attack. I took myself off to the library and looked for books. There was a whole shelf of them to choose from so I went with the one that had been borrowed the most: *Live a Life Free from Panic* by Sue Cotterill. The attacks kept coming, but the book did help, I learnt to cope with them better. The threat doesn't go away though, the threat is always there, and even when there hasn't been an attack for weeks you know one may be waiting in the wings. They are clever like that. You can't drop your guard because as soon as you do, as soon as you think you are safe, an attack will charge at you from nowhere and leave you terrified and shattered. What I never understood was why other people had panic attacks. I had good reason but why do housewives and accountants and dinner ladies suffer? Not everyone can have done something as terrible as I had. What reduces normal people to shaking, quivering wrecks?

20

I had made a decision. I was going to help Jake. I primed Mum early; Saturday night I would be round at Tom Clarkson's, we were going to watch some films and I was going to stay over. She eyed me suspiciously.

'Who's Tom Clarkson?'

'A lad in my English class.'

'You aren't going to be drunk in the park?'

I shook my head. 'He has some new films he wants to watch.'

'I didn't think you were one for films.'

She meant she didn't like me watching films. She thinks they are all loud and stupid and violent.

'I like films,' I said.

She was unsure, but didn't argue further, it was done, and I'd booked myself Saturday night away from the house. Saturday afternoon I met Jake at the playground and gave him his instructions for the night.

I packed a small bag with some essentials. I'd bought some chocolate biscuits and drinks to see us through the night because who knew what she had to eat and drink in the house. There was a tricky moment just before I was leaving. Mum came up to my room and said she wanted a number for Tom Clarkson's house, in case of emergency. My brain worked quickly and I told her that they only had mobiles and I didn't know the numbers. I got away with jotting down a house number and a street name and said a silent prayer that no emergencies occurred.

It was a close, muggy evening and even though the sun wouldn't be setting for a few hours, the threat of a thunderstorm hung in the air and heavy clouds darkened the town. As I headed away from our house there was a deep rumble over the other side of Denple Hill, and I thought about the town we'd left behind eight years ago and wondered if the same thunder had visited them too. It had been a hot day, and normally by now the town would be cooling down, relaxing into the evening, but the heat was trapped by the clouds and clung to the streets. Suddenly I felt uneasy about it all. The tension in the air added to the tension in my shoulders and I was on the verge of letting the panic win. I had to breathe deeply and slowly to stop an attack from mounting.

As I got closer to the town centre there was the odd spot of fat rain falling and I thought about the impact of rain. Would rain make her give up on her night out and stay in? I didn't think so. I thought she needed her Saturday night and her thick-necked man in his black shirt too much. The rain never quite breached the clouds anyway. Splat, splat, splatter and then nothing. I was at the steps by the dentist's for seven and sat and waited. It wasn't long until the street became busy and I even recognised a few faces from the time before. Some of the ladies were re-arranging themselves as they walked along, making sure that dresses were pulled up at the front and down at the back. The men were in short-sleeve shirts or T-shirts, despite the threat of rain. Tanned arms as thick as babies' heads were on show, stretch-ing the material out to busting point. I contemplated my puny arms and wondered if they could ever end up as wide as those out on the streets below. It seemed impossible. She was earlier this time, I saw her about half seven. Different dress, same handbag, same small, fast steps. As soon as the back of her head disappeared into the black of the Social en-trance I was up and off.

I started to feel good during the walk across town. I was out. Out for the whole night. We'd have a great time, do whatever he wanted, and then he could have an early night and a proper sleep. He could wake up feeling refreshed for a change, a brighter morning in front of him. The streets were quiet now. People were either already out or settled in for the night. A breeze had finally prised its way underneath the clouds and was working its way through the town. It felt good on my neck and underneath my shirt, and the sweat on my back began to cool. Fifteen minutes after I left the dentist's step I turned onto Fox Street. I walked a few yards until I reached the gravel track that ran behind the houses. I followed the track and walked to the back of Jake's yard. I closed the yard door quietly behind me, stood still and listened. Some of his neighbours' windows were open, the houses trying to lure the breeze, but the breeze not yet worked up enough to leave the streets and move indoors. There was Saturday night TV noise coming from the house on the right: laughter, clapping, whooping, a split-second silence and then noisy adverts. I felt safe stood there. The yard walls were high so nobody could see me unless they were in one of the back bedrooms of the adjoining houses looking directly at the spot I was stood. But there was nobody at the back bedroom windows on a Saturday night, nobody looking. I took the few steps to the back door and pushed the handle down. It didn't budge. I tried again, pushing the handle harder this time, but the door wasn't for shifting an inch. I was angry for a second. I'd told Jake. I'd told him all he had to do was say nothing and unlock the back door after his mum had gone and everything would be perfect. I caught myself. I was being silly. He was just a little lad. My anger left me quickly. It would be too early for him to be in bed so I knocked on the back door until a small, distorted figure appeared through the frosted glass, making his way forward. The lock clunked and he pulled open the door and I squeezed in.

At midnight the storm finally hit. I knew it was on its way because the clouds had dropped even lower, the air had thickened and there was nowhere for all the energy to go so it had to turn in on itself to fight a way out. Just like Mum and her silences. We were up in Jake's room, the light was off and I was stood close to the window watching the storm accumulate, enjoying the drama of it all. Jake was in bed, fast asleep, not making a sound. We were safe and dry and the weather couldn't touch us. The weather couldn't touch us until the first bang went off. It sounded like the belly being torn from under the town. Jake shot up with the force of a jack-in-the-box. 'What was that?' His eyes as wide as his old friend Harry's.

'It's thunder,' I said. 'It's a storm; it's going to be noisy. Do you get scared?' I could tell, looking at him, that he was scared, terrified, in fact. I moved over to the bed and sat down and told him to lie back. 'There's nothing to be frightened of,' I said, just as another panel of thunder dropped and shook the street. His face told me he didn't believe me, and I understood; this was some of the loudest thunder I'd ever heard and I was sure that to an eight-year-old it could sound like the world was ending. I thought it best to distract him. Distraction: a panic attack technique. I told him all I knew about thunder, that whilst it might sound horrible, it's only the sound of lightning, and lightning is just electricity in the at-mosphere. It didn't have much effect; he lay there, still terrified, looking up at the ceiling, then across to the window, dreading the next explosion. 'Do you ever daydream Jake?' I asked. He wasn't listening, he was too intent on what was going on outside. I took hold of his hands and told him to close his eyes and breathe slowly. I asked him what he wanted to be when he was older. 'Astronaut,' he said, without hav-ing to think. Just like me back then. 'OK. Imagine you've done all the training. You've been preparing for months. You're walking to the space shuttle with your helmet under your arm. And then you're in the shuttle and you're strapped in.' Another wall of thunder hit and Jake flinched. I told him to keep his eyes shut, to concentrate on what I was telling him. 'You're in the shuttle Jake and they're counting down to lift-off. You can hear the roaring and the shuttle is shaking and then you're leaving the ground and pushing up into the sky.' He gripped my hands tighter. 'The whole spaceship is shaking and the noise is huge and your head is wobbling like it might explode and then, suddenly, it's calm and quiet and you're cruising through space.' A flash of lightning lit up the room, I kept going. 'You unstrap yourself and now you're floating in the spaceship. You're doing slow-motion somersaults and swimming through the air.' I described the planets as he sailed past them. I described Earth as it faded away to the size of a blue full stop. Looking at him there I could see myself eight years ago, my bed a spaceship, vanishing into space, dying to escape. Slowly the storm began to move away and Jake's hands relaxed in mine, his face softened. The thunder was rumbling more than exploding now. I started leaving gaps between descriptions, there was no reaction from him, and I could see he'd fallen back asleep. He was flat on his back, nose pointing to the ceiling. I let go of his hands and placed them at his side. I caught his tiredness quickly and curled up at the bottom of the bed, just meaning to rest my eyes, to be close if the storm returned, but I was too tired and fell asleep myself.

I woke up feeling nervous. I checked my watch and saw it was half five and light out and the storm was long gone. I pulled myself up and sat down next to Jake. I gently ruffled his head and he moaned and twisted. I said his name and he squinted at me. 'It's light now Jake, it's early in the morning, I'm going to head off.' He nodded and put his thumb in his mouth. 'Are you going to be OK now?' I asked. He nodded again, his eyes closed and he was back in the land of sleep again. I leant down and kissed his forehead lightly. He was warm and smelt of sleep. I looked down at him and wondered how he would have coped with the storm if I hadn't been there. I didn't want to leave him but I dragged myself away, down the stairs and down the hall, towards the kitchen and the back door, wondering where I could go until it was time for me to go home. I pushed open the kitchen door and she was there in front of me, asleep in a chair, her head resting on her hands on the kitchen table. The air in the room sour and thick. I didn't move. I rode out the panic that rushed my body. Before I decided what to do the head in front of me lifted up. Two unreadable eyes looked at me before the head dropped back to the hands. I stayed where I was, unsure what would happen next. I don't know how long I stood there watching her, looking for a sign of movement, but none came. I backed myself out of the room and out into the hall. I opened the front door as quietly as I could and closed it the same. I ran as fast as I'd ever run down Fox Street, away from Jake and his mum and their house.

I couldn't go home. It wasn't yet six and an early return would provoke questions and I didn't need Mum's attention all over me after what had just happened. I pushed open the door to the haunted house and leant back into it until it closed shut. My heart thumped and my legs wobbled. I stood against the door in the dirty old hallway and tried to calm down. It felt strange to be there at that time of day, to be there alone. And even though it was a battered, desolate house, where nobody had lived for years, it still had the hushed feeling of early morning. I walked quietly up to our room, crawled under the plastic table, curled myself up and prayed for a sleep that refused to come.

In the afternoon tiredness hit and I told Mum I was going upstairs to read. It was a heavy, deep sleep, and I woke groggy and in a dark mood a couple of hours later. Had she seen me? I know she'd seen me, she'd looked right at me, but had she *seen* me? I'd heard lads at school saying they couldn't remember anything because they were so drunk, but I didn't know how much of that was truth and how much was talk. I wished I'd been drunk at least once in my life so I would know how you felt, so I would know what you remembered and what you forgot.

21

The man didn't even look at me as he bagged the drink. I didn't expect to be asked for ID, people always think I'm older than my age because of my height, but it could have been a toddler stocking up with booze and they'd have got served the same. I carried the drink back to the haunted house, got settled in my chair and opened a can. I'd bought eight cans of lager and a bottle of gin. I wasn't sure if it would be enough, but I thought I could always go back for more if I needed it. I drank a can of lager quickly and felt nothing so I tried some of the gin, but it was like drinking petrol and the only way I could get it down was by mixing it into the lager. After the lager and gin together, it started to hit. But Jake's mum had been in a proper state when I saw her so I ploughed on to try and get to where she'd been. It didn't take long. I remember I went to the quarry. I remember I shouted to the moon that it was a big silver-faced bastard and thought that was funny. I don't remember how I cut my hand, I don't remember how I hurt my knee. I do remember trying to sneak back up to my room and getting caught by Mum and not being able to stop laughing as she shouted at me and slapped me across the head. I don't remember being sick out of my bedroom window but I know that I was because I was made to clean it up the next morning and the smell and sight of it made me sick again, and then I was cleaning up new sick on top of old. And at the end of it all I was no nearer to learning if Jake's mum would remember seeing me. The only thing I'd found out was when you drink like that, the next morning you feel like you've been poisoned and you want to die.

*

I couldn't stand not knowing. I would rather have been in an interview room, answering questions, than sat in my room at home wondering if every car coming down the road was a police car heading to the house. I hadn't gone to school, the way I'd felt that morning I wouldn't have made it to the front gates without being sick again, and Mum didn't even try and make me. In the afternoon I still felt terrible, but I needed to know what was going on. I set off to try and intercept Jake on the way back from school, to ask if his mum had said anything, but my head was a mess and my timing was all wrong and I got to the school just as the last few dawdlers were leaving, and Jake was long gone. I set off on his route, to see if I could catch him up, to see if he was at the playground, but it was hard to walk fast, every footstep sent a jolt of pain to my brain, a kick of queasiness to my stomach, so I had to slow down just to make the distance. As I was about to turn onto Fox Street I saw the police car parked outside the front of Jake's house. Right outside, no mistaking, no room for hope. I veered back onto Waddington Road, my legs suddenly drunk again. I headed to the river, to where me and Fiona had walked a few days before. I left the road as quickly as possible, crossed a field and walked down to the riverbank. I found a spot by a bend where the water chops its way around the corner. I dropped myself into the grass. I didn't think about anything. I watched the water hit the rocks and negotiate its way around the turn. Groups of gnats lowered themselves over the water and flickered together like TV static. A brown fish launched itself into the air and hung for a second before dropping back into the water. I'd been there at least two hours before I finally got up to leave. I felt strangely calm as I walked through town and home. It was like I'd reached a conclusion somehow. It was a warm night and people were out and a friendliness hung over the place. Dogs gave me an interested sniff as they passed, neighbours were chatting over hedges in front gardens, and windows and doors were open everywhere. I was reminded that I liked Raithswaite. That it had been good to me, considering. The terror edged its way back in before I turned the last corner to our house, but when I saw there was no police car in sight I knew I had a while longer as a free man. I went straight up to my room and was in bed early. Before I drifted off I realised that these things could take a while. She didn't have a clue who I was and Jake didn't know where I lived exactly. Come to think of it, he didn't even know my second name. They would be coming, I was sure of that, but they hadn't worked me out yet.

22

When nothing had happened by Thursday I didn't
understand. I knew the bullet was speeding through
the air but didn't know when it would hit. My stomach was a mess; I'd hardly eaten in four days and I
jumped at the slightest noise, the smallest provoca-
tion. I didn't see Jake in the library at all and I wanted
it over and done with so I dragged myself to the bullet to get it done. I planted myself at the end of a quiet
street on his route home from school and waited. I
half expected him to be walked home flanked by police, helicopters hovering, but he made his way down
the street alone as usual, his hands holding his rucksack straps, his bouncy step pushing him forward.
He saw me from a way off and speeded up. I couldn't
help the pleasure that gave me, to have him happy to
see me. I called out to him. He was walking fast and
I had to up my speed to walk with him. I asked what
the police had been doing round at his. He narrowed
his eyes and looked like he was trying to think back

to a time impossibly long ago. 'There was a police car parked outside your house on Monday, after school,' I reminded him. It was coming back to him now and he started to nod.

'They came because of the trouble. They asked me questions,' he said.

'What trouble Jake? What were they asking you?'

'They asked if I'd seen anything unusual.'

'And what did you tell them?'

'I told them I hadn't seen anything,' he said.

'Did your mum ring the police Jake?'

He shook his head. 'It was Mrs Holt next door,' he said.

'Why did she ring the police?'

'She was crying. They took loads, but she said it wasn't the money, it was the stuff she couldn't replace, like the letters from Mr Holt.'

'She'd been burgled Jake?'

'Yeah. She says she feels like her home isn't safe any more. She was crying at our house.'

'And that's why the police were at your house?'

'They were asking what was taken,' Jake said.

I wanted to hug him.

'Did your mum say anything to you after I'd been round Jake? Did she mention seeing me?'

He shook his head.

'So she didn't say anything to you on Sunday?'

'She wasn't well,' he said. 'She had a tummy bug and spent the day in her room and then at night we watched TV together.'

'And she didn't mention anything to you about anyone being in the house?'

He shook his head again. She was too drunk to know that a stranger had spent the night in her house with her eight-year-old son. The stupid cow. I didn't walk with him much further. I thought it best not to risk it. I turned to head home. I was hungry for the first time in days.

23

The next Saturday morning I decided to go to the library with Mum. I thought it would do us good to spend some time together, doing the things we used to do, and I wasn't seeing Jake until the afternoon at the playground. I wanted to try and repair some of the damage from the last few weeks. It wasn't just me being kind; she'd hardly spoken to me at all since my drunk night and it was hard work to live like that, in even more silence than I was used to, so I was hoping to make life easier for myself. I was expecting a cold reaction but she nodded straight away when I suggested I went with her. On our way across town I found out why she was so keen. I had to check that I hadn't misunderstood, but she repeated her words as clear as day. We were booked on the internet for half an hour from ten o'clock. After the half-hour was up we'd be charged so we would have to be quick. 'You'll have to work it, the internet, Donald,' she said, 'I haven't a clue.' It was a shock because she doesn't believe in computers, especially not in the library. The day after they first arrived she wrote a letter to the council telling them to think about all the books they could have bought with the money instead, and wasn't that what a library was supposed to be for anyway? But recently she'd heard a programme on the radio about the invasion of privacy and at some point the talk turned to the internet. 'They say they've filmed every street of every town in the country. That you can see it all on the screen in front of you. Every street, like you're there.'

My heart sank.

'I'd rather not see it,' I said.

She glared at me.

'Well you'll have to see it because you'll have to help me. I think that's the least you can do. And we won't go near Hawthorne Road, so don't get silly. I just want to see the town.' We walked on in silence.

It wasn't just Clifton I was keen on avoiding, it was the whole of the internet. The thought of it makes me uneasy. Nothing ever dies, nothing is ever left be or left to disappear. Fingers prod away, adding to it, making it bigger and bigger, like they are gathering sticks for a bonfire nobody ever lights. But what I really mean is that there is a memorial page to Oliver Thomas. I only looked once, but there he was, smiling back at me. His name across the top of the page, four photographs of his short, happy life underneath. At the bottom it said, 'Always loved. Never forgotten.' The dates of his life underneath, the years so close together it broke your heart. There may be other pages out there about him, news articles, that kind of thing, but I never found out because I shut the computer down and haven't looked for him since. That's why I don't go online; I know I could find him in a few seconds and I don't trust my fingers.

At the library we settled ourselves in front of the computer, Mum letting me take charge. Within a couple of minutes she was sat forward, her hand to her mouth, as we made our way down Moor Lane in Clifton. 'Stop,' she said after a few seconds, 'Jackson's is still there, look, just the same. And look on the right, Nettletons Jewellers too. It hasn't changed.' Her face was inches away from the screen, her eyes flicking from Jackson's to Nettletons and back again. 'Try King Street,' she said, and we turned the corner and walked slowly down King Street. Then I showed her that you could turn and look at shops and houses directly, and she glanced at her watch, rooted in her purse for a pound and told me to pay at the counter. When I returned she told me what she wanted. She wanted to see all of the town centre and then old friends' and enemies' houses. We went to the Watson house on Cross Lane first: 'They've still not replaced that garage door!' We went to the Fearnhead house on De Lacy Street: 'New curtains and front door.' She was nearly overcome when we did a turn down Rathbone Road and saw old Mrs Armer on the left-hand side of the screen, walking along, carrying her shopping. We made it up and down nearly every street in Clifton. With ten minutes of our time left I showed her how to work the mouse. I typed in the address and went to wait outside. She came out a few minutes later, her eyes damp at the edges, looking a little unsteady. 'Well,' she said, 'that was a blast from the past. Clifton as I live and breathe.' She was quiet on the walk home and quiet when we got back. She didn't even grumble when I left the house straight after lunch.

24

That afternoon Jake was a broody version of himself. He was as snappy and sullen as Mum on a bad day. We didn't head to the haunted house; we didn't even leave the playground. He appeared on the cliff edge of tears from the moment I found him. The tears did eventually spill over and become real when he took a tumble, but he wasn't crying because of the fall and he wasn't for telling me what was upsetting him. He was so short with me, so miserable and unwilling to be helped that I got annoyed with him. He didn't see that other people had problems too. He didn't realise that I didn't have to be with him on Saturday after-noons, that there was plenty of other stuff I could be up to. I had my books to read, Mum had asked me to varnish the shed, and I could always go and see if Fiona was down in the quarry. But here I was, making sure he was all right, doing the best I could for him. I tried to snap him out of his blackness, but nothing was working. When I suggested all sorts of things we could spend the afternoon doing he shook his head at everything I could think of. I was fed up of making all the effort, and he was so miserable that I asked him if he just wanted to go home, but he said that his mum wanted some peace and quiet so we had an unhappy afternoon mucking around in the wood behind the playground. I thought to myself more than once that if I wanted misery and sulking I could get it at home just as well. He kept asking what the time was, and when I told him it had gone five he ran off back home, no happier than when we'd met.

When I got home Mum was still quiet. No doubt still thinking about Clifton and everything she'd left behind. I took myself off to my room for some thinking of my own. Something was wrong with Jake. As I lay there on my bed I realised that it wasn't just that he'd been upset; he'd acted differently towards me. He'd been cool. Dismissive. He'd kept skulking off and I had to keep my eye on him not to lose him. And I did lose him at one point, when he'd snuck off into the woods, and it took me a while before I found him sat down behind that tree. The more I thought about it the more I realised that he'd been acting fed up with me. Like at school when the people you are with just want you to go away and make looks at each other, and you don't cotton on until you catch one of the looks and then you realise and you feel sick. My insides turned cold at the thought of it: Jake didn't want to be friends any more.

In bed that night I thought about it more and calmed myself down. Something was upsetting Jake but it didn't have to be anything to do with me. It could be something at home or school that wasn't right and that was why he'd been grumpy. He was a sensitive kid having a tough time and I had to be the grown-up, I shouldn't be the one getting upset over nothing. And if I could find out what the problem was I could probably help. I made it down to the school for the Monday lunch break. I hung back and waited for them to come out and play. I wanted to see how he was, to see if he'd improved at all. Eventually he charged out of the red door, quickly followed by Harry, and they ran to their tree in the corner and jumped around and laughed and looked to be having the time of their lives. There was no sadness to Jake at all. Harry whispered something into Jake's ear and Jake fell about laughing, like he'd just heard the funniest joke in the world. Harry put his arm around him then, pulled him close and whispered something else and Jake laughed even harder. Stupid little Harry had him in stitches. The silly goggle-eyed redhead who'd abandoned him to play football with the football lads was now making him laugh like a drain. I tried not to be angry with Jake but I couldn't hold it back. There I was, looking after him, giving him time, setting up the house, seeing he wasn't scared at night, and now he was bored with all that. And he was probably laughing with Harry about it. Laughing at stupid old Donald who had no friends of his own.

I didn't go back to school. I walked to our house and went up to the room and sat down. There was still some gin in the bottle by the chair, there were still some cans in a bag on the floor. I'd felt so drunk on that night that I was sure I must have drunk everything I'd bought, but there was enough left if I wanted another go. But I didn't want to cloud my thinking. I wanted to be able to see clearly, to try and understand what was going on. I started at the beginning and slowly worked through it all in my head. And then I began to see. Jake had been fine with it at first. He'd enjoyed the attention and the stories and the house. And when Harry had dumped him and his mum wasn't bothered and I'd looked after him, he'd been happy with that too. But since Harry had come back, since the popular lads had rejected him, something had changed. Thoughts started jumping in my head like fleas. The night I went to stay with him, to look after him, he'd locked the back door before I got there. I'd told him five times in the afternoon to leave it open or to unlock it if his mum locked it. He might be young but he's not stupid. And the day I went to see him, to check if his mum had said anything about a stranger in the kitchen, he'd seen me and speeded up – I thought he was pleased to see me, that he was rushing towards me, but now I understood that he was trying to get away. When he went into the wood, when I found him sat down at the foot of a tree, he hadn't just wandered off, he'd gone when my back was turned, he was hiding from me. I knew then, I understood what had been going on. Harry knew about me and the haunted house and Harry had poisoned it. Harry had made it all wrong. I was sure of it.

My upset grew throughout the week. It started like a fist hammering in my chest but then it spread into my blood and wouldn't go away. I thought I'd found something pure with Jake. I thought it was something honest and good at last. A little lad who needed someone and I could be that someone. I knew it didn't make any difference to what happened in Clifton, but it wasn't about that, I thought I was making a difference for Jake, that I was doing something good, something kind. And I liked him. He was fun. He was good for me. But now it had gone wrong. Saturday I wasn't going to bother with him. I was going to head up into the hills and walk up and down steep climbs until I was wiped out with exhaustion. And I did intend to get on the bus out into the country, but instead I was there again at the playground, waiting for him to show. I didn't wait on the bench as usual, I stood at the edge of the wood, at the bottom of playground. I was in luck – his mum must have wanted some quiet time with her new man again, and he did appear, his head poking around the bushes at the entrance. When he saw the coast was clear he wandered over to the climbing frame. I wanted to march over to him straight away but a couple were playing with two young ones over by the slide, so I hung back. If Jake made a run for it I didn't want to cause a scene. Luckily one of the kids banged his head and wouldn't stop screaming so the family packed up to leave.

Jake was sat at the top of the climbing frame. He looked weary when I came into view, like I was the toddler and he was the exhausted mum.

'Are you all right Jake?' I asked him.

'Yeah,' he said.

'Do you want to do something?'

He shrugged. 'I was going to go home now.'

'You just got here.'

He shrugged again.

'That's a shame,' I said. 'Because I was going to tell you what happened at the haunted house.'

'Right.'

He wasn't interested.

'The other week, I was up there alone, sat in our room, and I saw her. I saw her right in front of me. The ghost woman.'

He was still acting bored, but he must have been interested a little at least, I was sure. I didn't say any more though. I waited for him to join in. He had to make some effort at least.

He tried to sound sceptical.

'You didn't see her.'

'I did. She walked right into our room, stopped and looked down at the floor, fell to her knees and let out a wail. I was so scared then that I ran out of the room and down the stairs.'

'You *did* see her?'

'Right there in front of me.'

'Did she see you?'

'She wasn't interested in me. She fell to the floor and started to groan.'

'It was probably where she got shot.'

'She *was* over in the corner where the bullet came through.'

'And you were scared?'

'I was terrified Jake. It was the sounds she was making, the noises coming out from her mouth were horrible. I've never heard anything like it. You would have been scared.'

'I wouldn't have been scared.'

I did his sceptical look back at him.

'Have you been back? Have you seen her again?' he asked.

'I'm not going there again.'

A fragile silence hung between us. Then, finally,

'Do you want me to come?'

'You wouldn't be able to scream, we don't know what she might do if she heard us scream, if we drew attention to ourselves.'

'It's OK,' Jake said. 'I'm not a baby, I won't scream.'

We walked out of the park and straight to the haunted house. I tried to chat to him as we went, but he wasn't interested. All he wanted to do was get to the house, see if there was a ghost there, and then, when there wasn't, get away from me. I was hoping that if I got him back in our room he might be reminded of the fun we'd had, and it might be like things used to be again, back when he was happy to see me, back in the early days.

It was a grey day, as dark as a day in December,

and the house sat back under the trees looking as haunted as it had ever looked. I felt hopeful for the first time in days.

'It's been a while since we've been here, hasn't it Jake?' I said, as friendly as I could. He didn't say anything. He went first and I followed. Inside it was even darker than usual. Jake wasn't bothered; he strode through the shadows, a little man with no fear. He did pause, just for a moment, before he went into our room, but you had to be watching him closely to see that. He walked to the middle of the room, scanned the four corners, looking for a ghost that didn't exist, and turned to me for an explanation.

'We have to give her a chance,' I said. 'She won't turn up right now just because we want her to.'

He looked around the room again.

'I don't believe you saw her,' he said.

'Why don't you sit down in your chair for a while and we'll give her time to show? I've brought some books,' I said, 'to pass the time.'

'I don't read books any more.'

'You don't read any more? Don't be silly Jake.'

'I don't. I'm bored of books.'

I started to get them out of my bag anyway. It gave me something to do. I didn't like how he was behaving. He was acting cocky and stupid, like one of the idiots at school.

'I don't think this is a haunted house,' he said. 'I think you're a liar. I think you made it all up to get me here.'

He looked right at me and said, 'I think you're weird.'

We stared at each other.

He rallied himself.

'Harry says you're probably one of those bad men.'

The house was silent, all sound sucked away by his words. I took one step towards him and his face ran over with panic. He sprinted past me to the door and was halfway down the stairs before I was after him.

I was slow. My legs were wobbly and cold, as useless as water. He was gone by the time I made it out of the back door and into the garden. I ran to the wall at the bottom of the garden and saw him, his blue jumper giving him away, over in the quarry, still running fast. Up and down he went, up and down over the steep little hills. I ran into the quarry and to the top of the steepest mound I could find. I shouted that he should stop being silly, that he should come back. The only reply was my own voice bouncing back at me from the tall quarry wall. But then I saw him.

That blue jumper was as good as a flashing light. I went after him again.

I found him hidden in a bush. I wasn't stupid, I didn't go charging in. I waited outside and tried to talk him out. I told him that he was being silly, that I would never do anything to hurt him and I was upset that he could even think that. Then, when he didn't reply, when he didn't appear, I said I could wait there all day, I could wait all night if need be. He took me by surprise. He charged out of the bush and walloped me on my shin and sprinted off. He got me right on the bone and the pain felled me. But I was quicker to get going this time and I was stumbling and limping after him again in seconds. I lost him down one of the many tracks, behind one of the little hills. I headed back to the top of the mound to see if I could get a sight of him anywhere. I shouted his name again, and again there was no reply. I began to panic. I'd never known him so determined. I scanned the quarry over and over but there was no sign of him. When I finally spotted him it knocked me cold. He was ten feet off the ground and making his way up the northern wall of the quarry, climbing like a spider, desperate to escape.

I was below him in less than a minute. I shouted for him to come down. He didn't answer. He was concentrating too hard, planning his route. He was a good climber, and he was doing well, but this wasn't a tree in a back garden and he wouldn't be able to make it to the top. I carried on shouting for him to stop, telling him he had to come back down, but he didn't reply and continued pulling himself further up. What terrified me was that he didn't have a clue how easily he would smash if he fell. He was too young to know that he'd crack like an egg if he slipped and dropped into the quarry. All I could think of when I saw him up there was Oliver Thomas, already dying by the time I left him. And it was that thought that made me go after him. But I'd only got about five feet off the ground when he looked down and saw me coming. He panicked and sped up, nearly slipped and let out a scream. I let go of the wall and dropped back to the ground.

'I'm not coming Jake,' I shouted. 'I'm not coming up. You have to be careful and slow down.'

But he'd stopped moving altogether. His left leg was stuck out awkwardly and his hands were high above his head. I could hear him crying.

'I'm stuck!' he screamed.

'I'm slipping!' he screamed.

'Jake, I'm coming now. You aren't slipping. Stay where you are, don't move. Just look at the wall in front of you.' He looked down and screamed again. There was terror in the strangled noise coming from his mouth. I threw myself into the wall and climbed as fast as I could, shouting up to him, trying to keep him calm. I would reach him, get him down safe, and he would see that I was a good person, that I was only ever trying to help. It might make everything better again.

'Jake, just look at the wall in front of you. Just stare at the wall in front of you and hold on.'

'I'm dizzy!' he shouted. 'I'm dizzy. I'm slipping. I'm going to fall! I am!'

He screamed again. I was moving as fast as I could, scrambling, climbing, pulling myself up to him. I could see the soles of his feet up above me to my left. Three more moves and I would be next to him. Then came another scream. He fell. He dropped past me in a moment. He hit the quarry wall further down and bounced back out and landed on his side in the quarry. He didn't sound like an egg cracking. He landed with a thump.

I stayed until the ambulance men came. I had to leave him to phone but I ran back and I was with him. We held hands. He tried to sit up, but cried out with pain, and was sick and there was some blood in the sick. He looked ten times worse than Oliver

Thomas had ever looked. I made him lie still. I kept standing up to see if any help was coming, but every time I stood up he started to cry and I had to get back down quickly to be with him. Finally I heard them shout, voices calling out for us, and I shouted as loud as I could, 'We're here! We're here! We're here!' but the last time I shouted it I was already not there and running away, trying not to hear Jake crying. The last thing I remember seeing is Jake lifting his head to see where I was, and the blood in the dirt on the ground and knowing that I'd been right all along: there has to be evidence left behind when something terrible has happened.

25

I bought a ticket and boarded a bus. I don't remember the journey. I came to when we pulled into a dark shady place and the driver turned the engine off and the bus rattled into silence. I got off with everyone else and followed them out of the bus station and into daylight. I recognised where I was from photographs and TV clips, but I'd never been there before; I'd never been in a city before. I walked past shops and glass buildings and tall old buildings, people everywhere. Not like Clifton, not like Raithswaite. It was too much of everything and I went back to the bus station. There was stand after stand and signs with letters and numbers on them and I couldn't make out how any of it worked. I asked a man in a fluorescent vest which bus went to Clifton and he said, 'Read the board lad, read the board,' and pointed to a huge perspex timetable cemented into the tarmac. I stood in front of it and all the numbers, times and destinations swarmed together like an army of flies that wouldn't stop moving and I thought for a second that I might pass out.

'Stand D, love. Twenty past the hour.'

I looked down at a middle-aged lady. I didn't know what she was saying to me. 'Clifton love.' She pointed behind me and said, 'Stand D. Twenty past the hour.'

'Thank you,' I said. 'Thanks.' And I don't know what my face was doing because she reached out and put her hand on my arm and said, 'Twenty past the hour love,' and tugged my sleeve before walking back to wait for her own bus.

An hour into the bus ride I saw an ivy-covered bridge over a train line, a broken barn in a field, a bicycle shop at the end of a row of houses. These places belonged to a time that didn't quite exist any more, half-memories stirred. Slowly buildings and streets began to look more familiar, I understood where I was, and then, finally, the bus stopped in the centre of Clifton. I stepped off and headed in the direction of Kemple Street. I wanted to approach the house from the same direction I had done the morning it happened. At the top of Kemple Street I found the track that cuts through to Hawthorne Road. It looked just as it always did, weeds and grass, potholes and grey gravel. I walked out of the end of the track and back into my childhood, all of it in front of me, like it had been waiting. I started down the hill. I passed Mr and Mrs Dawson's, Mr and Mrs Jackson's, old Mrs Armer's, some houses different, some just the same. Things are supposed to shrink when you get older. Nothing was shrunk here. Everything as it was. Then I was there: number seventy-five. They'd built a room over the garage. Probably an extra bedroom or a study, maybe a games room. People had those. The doors and windows were new, but you could still tell, it was still our house. I turned away and carried on. Mrs Franklin's, Mr and Mrs Seedall's, Mr Mole's, Mr Taylor's. Further down to houses where I didn't know who had lived there, not even by sight sometimes. The numbers were getting smaller now, my steps slowing. Then, finally, nine, seven, and five. I started looking from number nine. Just in case. My eyes to the floor, staring. *Come on*, I was thinking, *come on then, show me, show me.* I walked up and down, up and down, but the eight-year-old me was right. There wasn't a spot of blood anywhere.

26

Over the years two distinct memories have emerged, formed and sharpened. Both are as real and separate to me as my own two hands. In both memories I am riding my bike, that is the constant, it was me on my bike. I'd had it for nearly a year by then, still couldn't believe it was mine. In the first recollection it was early Saturday morning and I'd been riding around on the waste ground behind our house, but every time I passed the garage where the trouble with the kitten happened I felt guilty, so I rode to the front, onto Hawthorne Road. It wasn't as much fun there, there were less bumps, less space, but no bad memories. I was only allowed down to number sixty-five because Mum could see that far from the front window, and she knew Mr Taylor who lived there. But after Mr Taylor's the hill really starts to fall steeply and that was where you could get your speed up. By the time I'd raced down the steep slope, leaving number sixty-five behind a couple of times, it didn't feel like I was really breaking the rules any more. I was getting faster too. Braver each time. When the handlebars started to wobble, instead of holding tighter and reaching for the brakes, I'd learnt to relax my grip and ride the bumps out, to let the jolts and shocks dissolve into my arms and fizz away into nothing in my elbows. I looked at my watch, I had ten minutes before I had to be back inside. There was enough time for one more really good ride and I decided I would make the most of it and get to the bottom of Hawthorne Road for the first time by myself. I thought I could just about do that and get back in ten minutes, get back before I was in any trouble.

I started from outside my house and pedalled hard until I hit number sixty-five, after that I coasted for a while because it was impossible to keep up with the speed of the wheels anyway. I slowed myself for number thirty-seven because the pavement kinks to the left and you can't be going full tilt there or you'll end up in the road. After thirty-seven the pavement straightens out again, and if you put some serious pedalling in, you can get back up to speed in no time. I wasn't going the fastest when I hit him. Probably about eighty per cent. The main road at the bottom was approaching, so I would have started to slow a little, not much, but a little. I was still going fast. I saw a shock of blond hair appear from a gateway on the left, he was almost already under the wheels, and then I was no longer holding my handlebars, I was tumbling through the air. The pavement was the sky. The sky was the pavement. I landed hard, folded over like a piece of paper. I was sore and confused. I moved different body parts but nothing was screaming in pain; nothing was broken. I stood up. I was facing the opposite side of the road – the big grand houses with the steps leading up to their wide front doors wobbled in front of me. I turned to see what had happened but I was dazed and turned the wrong way and was looking at the bottom of the road. I managed to get myself the right way round and saw him lying there. Blond hair. A dark blue all-in-one outfit. Pink feet. No shoes. My bike was next to him. I ran back and knelt down in front of him and brushed the hair away from his eyes. His eyes were open. He looked curious. He looked deep in thought. I picked him up. I stood him on his feet, he fell forward into my legs and wrapped his arms around my knee. He wasn't crying. I crouched down in front of him and he tried to hug my face and I gave him a big hug back. 'Are you OK? Are you all right? Are you OK?' I kept saying into his face, looking for any damage. I pulled back to get a proper look at him. He pushed his hand at my nose like it was a button he wanted to press. I gave him another hug and then I took his hand in my hand and walked him to the open gate. He held onto my hand tightly. He stumbled once as we walked up to the house and he was wheezing, like he had asthma, but everything seemed to be in working order. There were no cuts or bruises, none that I could see. His hand was very warm. I jabbered as I walked with him, 'Are you hurt? God I walloped you then didn't I? Did you see me fly through the air?' The front door was ajar. It was a red door with a silver letter box. I was about to knock when I heard the shouting. Two of them at it, upstairs. Angry as Mum on a terrible day. There were words I'd never heard used before tumbling into my ears, words I instinctively knew must be the worst in the world. They were raging. I held my hand ready to knock, waiting for a pause, but when one of them finished the other started and then they were both going together. When there was finally a silence I got one knock in before the woman screamed like something was being torn away from inside her and I couldn't knock again after that. He'd gone floppier now and was leaning into my legs so I turned him round and sat him against the wall next to the front door. I knelt down in front of him and held both his hands and he smiled at me. 'Sorry,' I said. He smiled again and his head fell to one side and his eyes closed but he carried on smiling. I heard someone banging down the stairs then. I was terrified. I turned and ran. I reached my bike and clambered on. The steering was knocked out but I could still work it. I pushed down hard and pedalled back up the hill, trying to get back home before Mum spotted that I'd gone further than number sixty-five.

The other memory is just as clear. I woke up determined to paint. After breakfast I gathered all my stuff together and set myself up on the kitchen table. I spread out the old newspaper underneath, just like I was supposed to, and began to work. I leant forward to wash my brush in the water, but it was a long stretch and I was clumsy. I knocked the jar over. I rushed to clean it up but Mum heard the clatter and came charging in from the front room. I hadn't even noticed at that point, but it was the first thing she saw – the murky water had reached and covered her purse. She picked it up, water dripping from it. She threw it down on the table, took three fast steps and slapped me across my face. She screamed at me to get out and started to cry. Why is *she* crying? I thought. My cheek was throbbing, I could feel the skin pushing itself out in shock and pain, hanging heavy. 'Out! Out! Out!' she screamed, when I didn't move as fast as I should. I left the mess on the kitchen table and tumbled out through the back door. I took my bike from the yard and set off shakily. The air met my cheek and cooled the skin a little. I was shocked and rode slowly and wobbly with no destination in mind. She'd never hit me like that before and it took a while before I could think straight. As the shock lessened the anger started to come through and I rode past sixty-five, pleased to break her rules. All I'd done was knock some water over, her purse wasn't *ruined*, it would clean up. Why did she whack me so hard? Why was *she* crying? I was heading down Hawthorne Road, still not pedalling fast, but the slope was carrying me away and I was speeding up regardless. The anger reached my legs at the bottom of the slope and I started to pedal then. My cheek began to burn again, my legs ached and I was flying. Leaving that fucking woman behind. As I sped along I saw him step out from the front gate into the middle of the pavement. Just when I should have braked and pulled up I pushed down on the pedals – push, push, push and I hit him hard. I didn't hang around. I looked him over, saw there was no blood anywhere and jumped on my bike. I was away in seconds.

27

The truth is in those two accounts somewhere, but I can't get to it. I was eight years old when it happened and I've thought about it so many times, reimagined it over and over, and now I can't get to the truth of what happened. I know what happened afterwards, I got the details of that. His mum found him. She noticed the front door was open, thought of Oliver, ran out and found him sat against the house. He tried to get up when he saw his mum and that was when he collapsed. The ambulance must have arrived with its siren off. I didn't hear it and neither did Mum, but it made sense that it arrived silently; there wouldn't have been much traffic to clear from Clifton roads that early on a Saturday morning. I wasn't told when he died. I don't know if it was in the ambulance, in the hospital, or if he was already dead when I was halfway up Hawthorne Road on my way home. They did tell me that it was internal bleeding. I'd hit him so hard that the damage on the inside was too much for him to survive. That shocked me. In both memories when I hit him it was like riding into a tiny mountain, a little lump of hard rock, and it was me that was sent flying, my steering that was knocked out. Something as solid as that on the outside shouldn't crumble so easily on the inside. It was a catastrophic design fault. And if there was so much damage on the inside, how come none of it spilled out? How come it all stayed put inside? How can a chunky little two-year-old boy die so easily? So cleanly?

Eight years later I was no nearer an answer. I looked to the ground again but there was still no blood; still no evidence that any of it had ever happened. I noticed somebody watching me through a window from the house next door to Oliver's and I came to. I realised I didn't know how long I'd been stood there. I started to walk back up Hawthorne Road, past the kink in the road, up the steep stretch, the house numbers slowly crawling back up through the fifties and sixties. I wasn't thinking what to do next. I wasn't thinking of anything. I was getting closer to our old house and when I looked up I saw him leaning on his green wooden gate, watching me as I approached, his thick, heavy hands dangling over the side. As I got closer I realised it was Mr Mole. I couldn't believe that he was still alive; he'd seemed so old to me all those years ago, but there he was, looking no older by a day than he had back then. I stopped when I reached him. We looked at each other and he said, 'It's little Donald Bailey isn't it? From number seventy-five.'

I looked down at him and he smiled up at me and said,

'Little!'

The house was the same. Maybe the carpet was different but I couldn't be sure. I remembered that he decorated a room a year, but he never changed the colours, so nothing ever looked too old, but nothing ever really looked new either.

We were sat in his front room with a cup of tea each.

I looked around. 'No Scruffy?' I asked.

He shook his head. 'He went not long after you left,' he said. 'I keep thinking about getting another one, but I can't quite take the plunge.'

He blew on his drink.

'How's your mother?' he asked.

'She's all right.'

'Tell her I send her my regards.'

The clock out in the hall chimed, a cloud covered the sun and the room fell dark.

'Does she know you're here?' he asked.

I shook my head.

'I didn't think so.'

He shook his head back at me.

'I always thought it was a shame,' he said, 'that she whisked you away like that. I understood, but it didn't seem right.'

I looked at the floor. After eight years I was finally with someone who knew all about it, someone who would probably be happy to talk about it, and I couldn't say a word, wanted to keep it eight years away.

'Anyway Donald, how old are you now?' He put his head on one side and closed one eye and did some calculating.

'Fifteen is it?'

'Sixteen,' I said.

'Sixteen! And how are you? How are things? What brings you back here?'

I didn't know how to answer. All I could think of was Jake in the quarry and the patch of blood and the scream he let out when he fell. We sat in silence for a minute before he sprang into action.

'Wait there Donald,' he said.

He disappeared upstairs and I could hear him rummaging away up there, opening wardrobe doors, shuffling through drawers. A few minutes later he came back into the room holding an old plastic spaceship across the palms of his hands like he was presenting me with a medal, a big grin plastered across his old face. 'Do you remember this Donald? Do you remember how much you loved it?'

He held it out to me and I took it from him and turned it over in my hands. It was a model of the space shuttle *Columbia*. Other than my bike it had been my favourite present, I'd taken it everywhere with me, never let it out of my sight.

'How come it's here?' I asked him.

'The last time your mum dropped you off, not long before you moved away, you brought it with you as usual, but you weren't in the mood for playing with it and I put it on the sideboard to keep it safe. Your mum turned up suddenly and took you back home and you forgot to take it with you. I kept meaning to drop it off round at your house but the next thing I knew you'd gone and nobody really knew where you'd gone to. I've had it here all these years.'

'Why didn't you throw it away?'

He shrugged. 'It didn't seem right. You loved it so much, I didn't have the heart. I'd forgotten all about it until a few minutes ago.'

I turned the space shuttle over in my hands. It was

the one thing that had shrunk. I remembered it being long and thick and heavy, like it contained the miniature workings of a real spaceship inside. Now it sat in my hands lightly, a cheap-looking toy, dated and faded.

'Whenever you came round, for about a year, you always used to have that with you. And books about space, do you remember?'

I did remember. I remembered my first vanishings to Neptune. My escape to space. I remembered staring out of my bedroom window at the night sky, knowing that the stars I could see might be dead already, but not quite grasping how that could be, not believing that it was possible. A thought stirred at the back of my mind.

'I always thought you were going to be an astronaut,' Mr Mole said and looked at me and smiled. I managed a smile back.

'So,' he said. 'You'll stay for some tea?' Before I had time to answer he was already up and walking off, and a minute later I could hear him chopping away. I sat back in the chair, closed my eyes and breathed in the smell of the room. The house was the happiest place I'd ever known and to be here like this felt like I was ruining it.

As I tried to eat something he said, 'Do you want

to ring your mum Donald? Let her know where you are?' I shook my head, and he smiled and said, 'That bad is it?' I tried to smile back but it was impossible. After he'd washed up I was ready to leave, I had an idea where I was going next, but Mr Mole said, 'The spare room can be ready in minutes Donald.' As soon as he said it my legs nearly gave way with tiredness and I had to sit down. I went to bed early and slept until lunchtime. Mr Mole insisted I had some food when I finally came downstairs. He left me to it and went out to work in the back garden. When I'd finished eating I went out and helped him for the rest of the afternoon, just like I had done years before. When it got to four I told him I'd better be on my way, I had somewhere I wanted to go. 'Let your mum know you're OK Donald. She'll be worried sick.' I nodded that I would and Mr Mole walked me to the front gate where we shook hands like men in a film. He closed the gate behind me and resumed his position with his hands dangling over into the street, watching as I walked down Hawthorne Road, back towards the centre of Clifton.

I asked at the library. A bus from Clifton would take me to a village called Hethersby, from there it was a three-mile walk. Most people drive, I was told. The bus took for ever, winding its way through vil-

lages, waiting at stops for ten minutes without anybody getting on. The driver turned to me and said,
'This is it, this is Hethersby' at one of the stops in
one of the villages. As soon as I stepped off the bus
I could see it. There was nothing else to look at; it
was massive, the only thing on the horizon. A huge
white satellite dish supported by crisscrossed scaf-
folding. An antenna in the middle of it all, pointing
to the sky. The Pilchard Telescope, finally. It didn't
look anything like a telescope. I set off walking.

· I found my way to the entrance, walked through
the car park and followed the signs to the visitor
centre. I tried the door but it was locked. A man
in a blazer with a walkie-talkie appeared and told
me it closed at five, but I could walk to the base
of the telescope, he said, walk the path around it.
He said that they locked the gates at eight, so I had
forty minutes. He pointed out which path to follow
and I set off walking again. No one else was around
that late so I stood alone, staring up at the telescope.
Faded boards with facts about Thomas Pilchard and
the telescope were spread out along the route. I
stopped at each one, but couldn't take any of the
information in, the words refused to add up to anything that made any sense. I stared at the telescope
again but could only see Jake lying in the quarry. My

legs felt weak and I sat down on a bench. Eventually an announcement crackled out of a speaker somewhere. The site would close in ten minutes, would visitors please make their way to the exit. I looked around and saw a wooden shelter over by a small clutch of trees. I walked into the trees. After a few minutes the man with the walkie-talkie appeared and walked the path around the telescope, whistling. He walked over to the shelter and peered inside. On his way out he picked up a little teddy that had been dropped in the grass. He looked it over and put it in his blazer pocket. He locked the gates behind him. I heard a car start up and drive off.

I moved into the shelter and sat down on the floor and looked over at the telescope. Massive and silent. Miles above the sky ended and space began and planets and stars existed. Somewhere up there Neptune was spinning, like it always had done. Nothing down here making any difference to anything up there. Dusk fell, the sky darkening, slowly at first, and then suddenly, the huge telescope fading impossibly away. I fell asleep easier than I thought I would but slept badly. I dreamt of falling boys, and broken boys. I woke at dawn when the birds started singing. It was worse than the morning I'd found out Oliver Thomas was dead. It was a long time before anyone arrived but eventually the man in the blazer turned up, walked around the path again, and ten minutes later opened the front gate. After half an hour visitors began to arrive. First through the gate was a man holding a little girl's hand. They approached the blazer man, the man explained something, the girl stood shyly at his side. He ruffled the little girl's head as he spoke. The blazer man crouched down and pulled the teddy out of his pocket and presented it to the girl. A smile raced over her lips, she took the teddy quickly, pulled it into her chest and wiggled. The men laughed and shook hands, the little girl was made to say thank you and they turned and walked back to the car park, the girl still clutching the teddy closely to her chest. I waited until a few more visitors turned up and left the shelter and walked to the exit. Nobody noticed me leave. I walked out through the gates, across the car park and onto the country road. I was in the middle of nowhere.

28

I shouldn't have pestered for the bike. And normally I didn't nag Mum for new things. I wasn't a pain like that; I knew we couldn't afford much. And I was easily pleased as a child – it never failed to amaze me that I could walk out of a library with a bag full of books for free. But something changed when I was seven years old, when I decided I must get my hands on a bike. I knew the chances were slim, that it was unlikely we would have the kind of money needed to buy a bike, but I longed for one in a way I'd never longed for anything before. I talked about it so much that Mum tensed at the mention of the 'b' word. She must have told a friend about the situation because one afternoon I was marched to the garage of an older boy's house and was told to sit on his bike, to see if it was a fit. The bike was too big for me, even with the seat as low as it would go, but not too big that Mum could turn it down at the price it was being offered. The sale was agreed, the garage door slammed shut, and I was told I wouldn't see it again until the morning of my birthday. I was delighted with the bike. The fact that there were dirty stickers stuck to the frame and the handlebar grips had long since started to wear away didn't bother me at all. That it was battered and too big didn't come into it. It was a bike and it was going to be mine. I finally gave Mum's ears a rest and waited impatiently for my birthday to arrive.

The morning of my birthday I was more excited than I'd been in previous years. I wanted to get out and start riding. Feel the wind in my hair. Ride along with the front wheel up in the air. Skid to a stop on the waste ground behind our house, scattering stones in my wake. Before any of that could happen I was called into the kitchen to eat my breakfast, which I wasn't even hungry for. 'The sooner you eat, the quicker you get your bike,' Mum said. I sped up and worked my way through the toast whilst Mum sat opposite fiddling with her camera. I should have guessed something was up when she followed me into the hall to the bike under the dustsheet with the camera in her hand. I lifted the sheet up and stopped mid-reveal. I was looking down at a new black tyre, shiny silver spokes and a bright red frame. No rust anywhere, no stickers or scratches, not a blemish in sight. I must have stared for a while because Mum became impatient and said, 'Come on then Donald,' and pulled the sheet from the rest of the bike herself. She uncovered a bright red, brand-new Raleigh. I was stunned. She took a picture of me, standing there staring, like I was seeing something I couldn't quite understand, but the next photograph must have been from a few minutes later when I'd come to a bit, and I'm stood holding the handlebars of my new bike, a beaming smile plastered across my face.

I was well aware that most boys and girls my age had been riding bikes for years before I got my hands on one. That was partly the reason I wanted a go. I'd watched them shooting up and down the street, chasing each other around, getting shouted at by neighbours, beeped at by cars. It looked great fun. What I hadn't considered was that a skill was required; that there was a knack to be mastered. I'd seen kids fly past my window and I wanted some of that. I wanted a go and I thought that once you got yourself sat on a bike, the battle was won. So after the euphoria of pulling the dustsheets off and discovering the new bike underneath came the disappointment when I realised I was completely unable to do anything with it. I wheeled the bike out to the track that ran down the back of our house and sat on it and had no idea what to do next. I lifted one foot off the ground and placed it on a pedal, and then as soon as I lifted the other foot up, the first foot shot back down to the safety of the earth. I must have done this over and over again for about twenty minutes. Riding a bike seemed as impossible as flying to me right then. I went back to the house and asked Mum how it was done, but she shrugged at the question and I understood, her part of the miracle had already been performed.

In the afternoon I hit on the idea of taking the bike round to the front of the house and using the kerb to help me along. I kept my left foot on the ground and pushed the pedal forward with my right foot. I shuffled the bike along and I was moving at least, and movement felt like progress. As my confidence grew I could do a couple of revolutions of the pedal with my right foot, lift my left foot off the ground for a couple of seconds in the knowledge that the kerb was close by to save me. By the end of the first day I could wobble my way forward for a good two pedal revolutions. I was out until the street lights buzzed on and Mum dragged me in. I was shattered at night, but I went to bed knowing that I was further on than I had been that morning. By the end of the second day I was riding in a wobbly line for a good few yards. Turning around had yet to be mastered and I couldn't see how it could be done, so each time I wanted to head in a different direction I dismounted and turned the bike to face the way I wanted to travel. But it came in time. When I finally managed a circle with no feet touching the ground it was a great moment. I'd taken my bike to the piece of waste ground at the end of the track behind our house and did the turn, which was so gradual it had the circumference of a cricket pitch. As my confidence grew the circles became tighter and faster and I made myself dizzy and had to sit down to let the spinning subside. Two weeks later I could skid and wheelie like any other kid. I spent most of that summer on my bike. I wasn't allowed to stray too far so it was mainly up and down the road to number sixty-five and down the back track to the waste ground behind the houses. I'm not sure what happened to the bike in the end – it didn't come with us to Raithswaite but I don't remember leaving it behind in Clifton either. I do remember that the police had it for a while. Maybe they never gave it back. Maybe it's still in a room somewhere in Clifton, covered in dust and rust with a faded evidence tag tied around the handlebars.

29

If I was in Iowa I would get up early. Walk the dog before work. Have a breakfast of eggs, coffee and orange juice with Lucy before jumping in the pickup and driving to the store. I would push open the door to the warm smell of wood and dust, make myself another coffee and get to work on the accounts at the counter. At Raithswaite police station there aren't any nice smells. There are two policemen, a man in a suit, my mum and me. We are all sat in a small hot room. One policeman is asking all the questions.

'How would you describe your relationship with Jake?'

'We were friends.'

'A sixteen-year-old and an eight-year-old boy?'

I nodded and said, 'Yes.' My voice didn't sound like mine. It was too high and scratchy.

'Did it not strike you as inappropriate?'

'I didn't think so.'

'Do you understand what "inappropriate" means?'

I nodded that I did.

'You spent a lot of time at the playground on his street?'

'Sometimes, yes.'

'Aren't you too old to be hanging around a playground?'

I didn't answer that one.

'Why this playground? It's nearly two miles from your house.'

'I walk all around Raithswaite. I go all over.'

'You go to all the playgrounds?'

'No. I go all over Raithswaite.'

'Sixteen-year-olds and eight-year-olds don't normally meet and become friends.'

I didn't know what to say.

'Did you approach him first?'

'I can't remember.'

'Somebody must have spoken to someone first. Today I spoke to you first. Who spoke to who first? You or Jake?'

'We just got chatting at the library one day. I saw him in the library quite a bit. He looked lonely. His mum was never with him, she never looked after him.'

'And this is what you were doing? Looking after him?'

'Sort of. Sometimes.'

'So you spoke to him first then, because he looked lonely?'

'Maybe. I can't remember exactly.'

'Don't you have any friends your own age?'

'Not too many.'

'Why is that?'

I thought about Neptune up there. All that space and silence.

'I don't know,' I said.

30

'What happened when he fell?'

'I was trying to help him. Trying to get him down, but he panicked and slipped and fell.'

'He said you were chasing him.'

'I was chasing him, but when he got into trouble on the quarry wall I was trying to help him.'

'Why were you chasing him?'

'I was trying to get to him, then I could walk him home safely. He'd gone silly and run off.'

'He says that you dragged him to the house to show him a ghost and he tried to escape and you went after him.'

'But he wanted to see the ghost.'

'The ghost that you'd invented. To get him to go to the house.'

My mum put her head in her hands. I wished I lived alone in a house on top of a high hill. I'd sleep in the attic. As close to space as possible.

'I only invented it for him. So he could have fun.'

'We've been in the house. We've seen your room.'

'Is he OK?'

'Did you set all that up? The table and chairs?'

'I didn't steal them.'

'But you put all that stuff in there?'

'Yes.'

'Why? What did you and Jake do there?'

'Read books.'

'You read books?'

'Sometimes. Horror books. He liked them.'

'You took an eight-year-old boy, walked him nearly two miles across town to an abandoned house and read him horror books?'

'Yes.'

He looked at me for a long time.

'Is he OK?' I asked.

'He's out of hospital now. Still battered and bruised.'

'Will you tell him I'm sorry?'

'What are you sorry about Donald?'

'That he fell and hurt himself.'

'And that's all?'

'I'm sorry he was scared.'

'Why was he scared?'

'He got silly thoughts in his head.'

'Silly how?'

I didn't know if I should say it.

'His friend had told him that I might be a bad man.'

'What type of bad man?'

'I don't know. But suddenly he didn't want to be friends.'

'And you were angry about that?'

'Not angry, sad.'

'But you were chasing him. A sixteen-year-old takes an eight-year-old to an abandoned house, to see a ghost that he's invented, and when the young boy gets scared the older boy chases him, so he thinks his only way to escape is to scale a sixty-foot wall. What are we to make of that Donald? How scared must he have been?'

'It wasn't like that.'

'What was it like?'

Whatever I could say to them would only make it worse.

31

It did get worse when they found out that I'd spent the night at Jake's house. I hadn't told them, but they must have spoken to Jake again and got it from him. It was lunchtime when a car arrived at the house and me and Mum were driven back to the station.

'You broke into the house and stayed in his room?'

'I didn't break in. He was scared of being alone.'

'So you were looking after him? Making him feel better?'

'Yes, I was. He wanted me to stay with him.'

'That's not what he told us. He told us that you turned up one night at the back door and you pushed yourself in.'

I shook my head. It wasn't like that.

'Did you force your way in?'

'I didn't push myself in. He let me in.'

'He told us that he was scared of you, that you wouldn't leave him alone.'

I didn't know whether to believe them or not. I

wished I could talk to Jake. I didn't think he'd been scared.

'Ask him about the storm. Ask him about the night of the storm. There was thunder and lightning and he was terrified and I stayed with him. I helped him fall back asleep.'

'How many times did you go to the house at night?'

'Twice.'

'Twice?'

'Yes.'

'Why do you not see how inappropriate that is? To turn up like that and spend the night with an eight-year-old boy.'

'But his mum wasn't there. She left him all the time.'

He stopped going at me for a second then and said,

'It wasn't your place to act on it. Not in this way. You should have told someone.'

'I was just trying to look after him. Trying to make him feel better.'

'Were you taking advantage of the fact that he was left alone?'

I shook my head.

'I was trying to make him happy.'

The detective looked at me. He didn't seem to know what he was looking at.

'How did you try and make him happy?'

'With the books, and looking after him when he was alone, and he loved the house, and sometimes we played outside.'

'And that made him happy?'

'Sometimes, I think.'

'Did you ever do anything else to make him happy?'

'I bought him cans and chocolates. Sweets. Played with him, read him stories.'

'Not like that Donald.'

He stared at me and I tried to stare back but I couldn't keep it up.

'No. I didn't do anything else to make him happy.'

He looked at me and I felt as guilty as if I'd touched Jake all over.

32

This time it was worse than graffiti on the door and lads shouting at the house. I tried not to go out much, and I wasn't going to school anyway, but sometimes you have to leave the house. I didn't know what was happening with the police, I was waiting to hear and desperate for something new to read, something to help me escape, so I went to the library. I got there without any trouble, but in the library, a place I'd been going to for years, I felt uneasy. I chose my books quickly, used the self-service machine and headed back home. Whenever I passed anyone, or anyone glanced at me, I knew what they were likely thinking and I wanted them to know that whatever they'd been told, whatever they thought about me, was probably wrong. It doesn't work like that though; you've just got to let them have their stare and think what they want. I started using the back alleys and side streets.

I was halfway down an alley behind Lime Street,

about half a mile from home, when I heard running feet behind me. Before I could turn around and protect myself, something hard and heavy smashed into the back of my head. It didn't hurt straight away but the force of it sent me to the ground. There were two of them. One kept smashing down on me with the weapon, the other used his feet. I curled up as much as I could and tried to wrap my arms around my head to protect myself, but it was like getting caught in a storm on a hillside where there's nowhere to go and nothing to do other than take what comes. I was scared at first but the longer it carried on the less I cared. After a while I blacked out. When I came to they had gone, but I wasn't sure I could move, and then I must have blacked out again because the next thing I remember a lady was crouched down beside me, rubbing my hand, saying, 'It's Sarah, love, Sarah from number twelve. Just stay still, stay where you are. I've rung for help.' She brought me a glass of water. I tried to drink but I couldn't tell where my lips ended and the glass began. As they lifted me up into the ambulance Sarah said she was sorry that she couldn't come to the hospital with me but she had to collect her children from school, there was nobody else could do it. I should have thanked her for helping but they closed the ambulance doors before I got the chance.

At the hospital nobody sat near me. I don't know what I'd rolled in in the alley, but I smelt terrible. Everything started to hurt more as time went on. There was a burning pain in my chest and the left-hand side of my torso turned from roasting hot to cold and back again in seconds. My right hand was a mess too. I was sure that something was broken. A nurse assessed me when I arrived but then I waited for two hours before I was seen properly. A man in blue trousers and top finally called out my name and led me down a corridor to a bed and pulled the curtain closed around us. Fingers were held in front of me and I had to say how many I could see. Different shapes and symbols were traced on my forehead with a finger and I had to describe what shape had been drawn. I was asked questions about what month and year it was. Then I had to get undressed and was examined all over before being X-rayed. When I came back out of the X-ray the police were waiting to talk to me, but I didn't want to talk to them. I'd caught a glimpse of the face of the lad who was bringing down the blows on my head. It was Tyler, Fiona's brother. I told the police I didn't see anything, that they'd attacked me from behind and I didn't see anything.

I lied about blacking out; I told the man in blue that I'd been conscious throughout it all so after they bandaged me up I was allowed to go home. I had two broken ribs and two fingers on my right hand were broken and there were bruises all over. I finally looked at my face in a mirror. It was swollen out of shape and looked like everything was sliding out of place. I was told I was lucky, with the extent of the bruising it could have been worse, they said. Pain rolled through my body and they gave me some pills for it. Nothing happened until I doubled up on the amount I was supposed to take and then they started to work. When I was discharged the man in blue said reception would ring a taxi for me, but I had no money so I said I would walk. They wouldn't let me do that and, when I told them there was nobody to pick me up, a nurse arranged for me to have a lift in an ambulance. I asked the ambulance woman to stop a couple of streets away so Mum wouldn't see, but she said they had to see me to the door. I snuck in and got lucky, Mum didn't see the ambulance or me, and I went straight to bed. The next morning I came down for breakfast. 'Look at you,' Mum said, and started crying. I felt terrible. There had been trouble for her too. Not fists and punches, but they might as well have punched her in the face the damage it did. And at least I had my vanishing to look forward to. I had an escape that I knew was coming. I'd ruined

Clifton for Mum and now I'd ruined Raithswaite too. I'd left her with nowhere to go.

I had somewhere to go. The vanishing came to me on the bus journey back to Raithswaite, after I'd spent the night at the Pilchard Telescope. It presented itself fully formed, like the best vanishings always did. It was a beautiful morning and everywhere people were smiling. Women fell in and out of conversation on the bus and looked out of the windows and watched the hills and villages as we rolled along. Out on the streets people waved to each other, walked their dogs, walked to the shops. Everyone looked comfy, they all looked like they were in the right place, doing what they were supposed to be doing. The vanishing appeared for me then. I suddenly saw my way forward.

33

I went back to see Jake. It didn't matter that I wasn't supposed to, that I could get in more trouble. I had to see him, I needed to check that he was all right, that they'd told me the truth. I waited in the trees outside the playground. My timing was out and I had to wait ten minutes before the yard started to fill up, but then I saw him. There were three of them now: him, Harry and another lad, a new friend, almost as gormless-looking as Harry. The weather had turned and there was a snap in the air, a cold that hadn't been in the town for months. Jake's two friends were wearing coats, Jake was only in his jumper, and I wondered if he even had a coat, I'd never seen one, he'd need something for the coming winter. Maybe a teacher would notice. The tree in the corner was still their spot and they headed over there and started to muck around, pushing each other, laughing and chatting. They looked like they were having fun and it was good to see. It was only when the other two ran off and Jake went after them that I noticed his leg. He dragged it along after him slightly, like he couldn't quite lift it all the way off the ground. It slowed him down, but it didn't look like it caused him any pain and he appeared to be having as much fun as the others, even if he couldn't quite keep up. To see him so firmly alive was the best sight I'd ever seen. After I'd watched him for a minute or two I turned to leave. I walked across town to the haunted house but I could see from the road that the police had been at it. There were grilles over the windows and round the back it was just the same: a grille over the door, all the windows covered, no way back in at all.

34

The only other person I wanted to see was Fiona. It was impossible to go to her house because of her brother, and I still wasn't going to school, so I had to keep my eyes peeled on the quarry. Finally I saw her. I didn't know how she would react but it was important to speak to her. I called out her name but her headphones were in and she was walking away from me. When I touched her shoulder she jumped and spun round. 'Bloody hell Donald. You scared the shit out of me.'

'Sorry.'

'Fucking creeping up on me like that.'

'Sorry.'

'God you look a mess.'

'I look better than I did.'

'They made a right mess of you.'

'I didn't know if you would talk to me or not.'

'What were you thinking Donald?'

'I wasn't doing anything bad.'

'The police came to ask me questions and I didn't know what to tell them,' she said.

'I wasn't doing anything funny.'

'I don't think you were.'

'Nobody else believes it though.'

She pulled out a pack of cigarettes and offered me one and I took it and we set off walking. We kept going until we came to the back wall of the quarry.

'How far did he fall?'

I pointed.

'Bloody hell.'

'There's talk about fencing it off at the bottom. So it can't happen again.'

We didn't stay there long. It made me feel sick. As we walked off I started telling her about Clifton and Oliver Thomas. She ended up coming into the house. We sat at the kitchen table and I carried on talking, I told her about it all. The two memories, everything I could think of, everything I could remember. Mum was in the room next door and must have known what was going on but she didn't try and stop me.

35

After I'd seen Jake and Fiona I was ready. On the night I decided to go I went up to bed at the usual time but kept my clothes on. I left the light on in my room and crept out of the house at midnight when I was sure Mum would be asleep. It was a clear night, the stars clustering and bright. I walked to Lime Street and pushed a thank-you card through the letter box of number twelve as quietly as I could. Then I walked back to Eastham Street, the big houses sat at the top of their drives, as silent as monuments. I cut through the woods where I'd carried the furniture for the haunted house and headed for the quarry wall. There is a tall wire fence to keep people away from the sudden drop, but I'd done my research and knew where it had been cut, where I could squeeze through. As I pushed through the overgrowth I saw a Portakabin behind some trees I'd never seen before. I tried the door but it was locked. I sat near the lip of the quarry. I had a few cans with me and I drank for a couple of hours, not a silly amount, not like last time, just enough to make me woozy. It was a beautiful night, as calm and peaceful as any of my vanishings had ever been. I stood and walked to the edge of the drop and looked down into the thick blackness below. You couldn't see the bottom, you couldn't see anything down there and I started to feel dizzy. I stepped back. I thought about Jake and Oliver and decided I would try not to think about them any more. I looked over the quarry to our row of houses. I could see the light from my bedroom window, a small light, the only light on in any of the houses, and realised how easy it was to walk away. Already I was far enough away from her that I couldn't hear, even if she shouted.

I'd filled my bag with clothes and I had some money I'd stolen from her purse. There wasn't much, but it was enough to get me to where I wanted to go. The first bus would arrive in the city about half eight, so I left the quarry at six to make sure I didn't miss it. There were three of us on the bus when we left Raithswaite, but by the time we pulled into the bus station people were standing in the aisle, holding on to bars and trying not to fall into each other as we turned tight corners. It was a relief when we pulled to a final stop and the doors opened and the bus

223

cleared. I had an hour before my next bus so I walked up and down the wide streets of the city centre. I felt much better than the last time I'd been there, but the place still scared me, and I kept getting in the way of people rushing along, striding hard, like they were racing each other. I tried to get out of everyone's way but wherever I walked somebody wanted to get past, and I was worried I wouldn't be able to find my way back to the bus terminal, so I didn't go too far, didn't explore too much, didn't want to miss the bus.

It was about a quarter to eleven when I knocked on his front door, but there was no reply, so I sat down against the house, waiting for him to return, hoping he hadn't gone away on holiday. After a couple of minutes I heard a snipping sound, coming from the back of the house. I picked up my bag and walked to the side gate and listened again and could hear it clearly now. He was working in the garden. I clicked open the gate and walked down the side of the house and saw him in the far corner, on his knees, sleeves rolled up, working on some stems. 'Mr Mole,' I said. But I was nervous and too far away and he didn't hear me, so I cleared my throat and spoke his name more loudly.

Acknowledgements

Thank you:

Antony Harwood, Julian Loose, Kate Murray-Browne, Alex Bowden, Jim Lee, James McGrath, Juliette Tomlinson and everyone at Faber.